"I haven't been pining away for Geneva, hoping for my next chance, if that's what you're worried about."

Jessie's gaze snapped to his. "What if Geneva weren't married?"

"But she is."

Jessie gnawed on her lower lip, silent for a moment. She'd imagined what it would be like to be with Gideon, even for just one night. To finally let go of all of the fantasies and what-ifs that kept her awake at night.

"Thank you for the dance, Gideon. But I should mingle with some of the other guests." Jess suddenly pulled out of his embrace. "And I need to check with Teresa to see if either Chase or Dixon has arrived."

"Of course." Gideon nodded, shoving a hand into his pocket. "I understand. But maybe we could have a nightcap later?"

Jessie stared into his dark eyes, her pulse racing. She wanted to accept his offer. To tell him exactly what she'd imagined so many times. But it would be a mistake.

* * *

Seduced by Second Chances is part of the Dynasties: Secrets of the A-List series.

Dear Reader,

Dynasties: Secrets of the A-List introduces us to the secrets and scandals of the wealthy players in the Emerald City—Seattle, Washington. Each book follows two couples.

In *Seduced by Second Chances*, we pick up on the on-again, off-again relationship between A-list event planner Teresa St. Claire and billionaire businessman Liam Christopher. Ugly rumors paint Teresa as a calculating gold digger who targeted the late Linus Christopher and now has her sights set on his heir. Can she convince Liam otherwise?

At an elegant art deco–style hotel situated on a Napa Valley vineyard, singer Jessie Humphrey encounters billionaire real estate developer Gideon Johns. He broke her young heart a lifetime ago and is the inspiration behind the songs she writes about devastating heartbreak. Has fate given Jessie a second chance with the only man she's ever wanted? Or will their painful history and high-stakes careers on opposite coasts be too much to overcome?

Thank you for joining me for this episode of Dynasties: Secrets of the A-List. To discover my Bourbon Brothers and Pleasure Cove series, visit reeseryan.com/desirereaders. For series news, reader giveaways and more, join my VIP Readers newsletter list.

Until our next adventure,

Reese Ryan

REESE RYAN

SEDUCED BY SECOND CHANCES

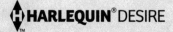

Special thanks and acknowledgment are
given to Reese Ryan for her contribution to the
Dynasties: Secrets of the A-List miniseries.

ISBN-13: 978-1-335-60375-3

Recycling programs
for this product may
not exist in your area.

Seduced by Second Chances

Printed in U.S.A.

www.Harlequin.com

Reese Ryan writes sexy, emotional love stories served with a side of family drama.

The 2017 *Los Angeles Times* Festival of Books panelist and 2018 Donna Hill Breakout Author Award recipient is author of the Bourbon Brothers and Pleasure Cove series.

Connect with Reese via Instagram, Facebook, Twitter or reeseryan.com.

Join her VIP Readers Lounge at http://bit.ly/VIPReaders Lounge.

Books by Reese Ryan

Harlequin Desire

The Bourbon Brothers

Savannah's Secret
The Billionaire's Legacy
Engaging the Enemy

Dynasties: Secrets of the A-List

Seduced by Second Chances

You can find Reese Ryan on Facebook, along with other Harlequin Desire authors, at Facebook.com/HarlequinDesireAuthors!

For all of the amazing readers who read and recommend my books, *thank you*! Your support is invaluable.

For Building Relationships Around Books (BRAB), Round Table Readers Literary Book Club, Victorious Ladies Reading Book Club and Sistas' Thoughts from Coast to Coast (STCC Book Club), thank you for hosting me for lively book discussions. I cherish the time spent with you and appreciate all you do to promote authors.

* * *

Don't miss a single book in the Dynasties: Secrets of the A-List series!

Dynasties: Secrets of the A-List

Tempted by Scandal by Karen Booth
Taken by Storm by Cat Schield
Seduced by Second Chances by Reese Ryan
Redeemed by Passion by Joss Wood

One

Jessie Humphrey scrolled through her cell phone contacts and located the number she was searching for.

Her dream list of world-famous producers was a short one, but Chase Stratton reigned supreme. He'd worked with the top talent out there. Single-name artists at the pinnacle of their careers and critically acclaimed artists on the rise.

Jessie paced her tiny one-bedroom apartment in SoHo and chewed on her fingernails. Her entire future was riding on making this happen.

She sank onto the living room chair where she did much of her songwriting.

Her record label had offered her a new contract. To her agent's dismay, she'd rejected the offer. The studio wanted her to make cookie-cutter pop music rather than the soulful songs about love and loss that were her forte.

She'd been writing for some of the studio's biggest stars for years. As an artist, she had two albums under her belt and a growing base of die-hard fans. Including wealthy, powerful people like Matt Richmond, who'd paid her a generous fee to perform at his exclusive event in her hometown of Seattle, Washington.

With her current recording contract fulfilled, Jessie was at a stalemate with the label's top exec, Arnold Diesman.

She'd taken Matt Richmond's gig in Seattle because of the lucrative contract. Money she would invest in starting her own independent label where she would retain creative control.

Chase had a long line of artists with household names and the deep pockets of the record labels backing them. But Jessie needed to convince him to take a chance on working on her indie project.

She'd called in every favor she had to track down the phone number of Chase's personal assistant. Jessie dialed the number.

"This is Lita."

"Hi, Lita, this is Jessie Humphrey. I sent a couple of demos to Chase—"

"We received them. Thank you. But Chase's schedule is booked solid right now."

"I'm not surprised. He's the top producer out there right now." Jessie was undeterred by the woman's attempt to blow her off. "I know I'm not one of the single-name artists he usually works with and that I won't have the backing of a big studio for this project—"

"You realize you're making a case *against* me passing your demo on to Chase, right?" Lita laughed.

"Just acknowledging the obvious." Jessie paced the hardwood floors. "But he should consider my growing fan base. They don't care whether a big studio is behind the album. They only care that—"

"Look, honey, not everyone can drop an independent surprise album that'll shoot up the charts. And it's unheard of for an independently produced album to be Grammy-worthy. I know Beyoncé and Chance the Rapper made it look easy, but it isn't. And Chase only deals in top caliber projects. Now, if you have your studio rep contact us…"

"My contract is over and I'm not interested in signing another. I want complete creative control." Jessie continued when the woman didn't respond. "I've written huge radio hits for Top 40 acts. I know what sells."

"Look, Jessie… I'm a huge fan. But Chase has much bigger projects in his sights. And without studio backing…" The woman lowered her voice. "There's a reason Chase commands such an exorbitant payday. He selects his projects carefully. He always wins because he only plays the game when he's holding a royal flush. I listened to your demo. The songs are amazing and so is your voice. But Chase isn't willing to take on the risk of working with you without the backing of the studio."

"I see." Jessie stopped pacing. Tears stung her eyes.

"I'll hold on to your demo. When Chase needs a new songwriter, I'll recommend you. Maybe once he works with you in that capacity, he'll take a chance on your indie project."

"If I could just talk to him myself—"

"Sorry, Jessie. This is the best I can do for you right now. Chase is preparing to work on the West Coast for the next several weeks. But I'll keep you in mind when he needs a new songwriter. Promise."

"Lita, wait—"

The woman had already ended the call. Jessie sat at the piano that took up most of the space in her living room.

She'd have to find another way to get face time with Chase.

Jessie was determined to make authentic music. She wouldn't be strong-armed by the studio into cranking out forgettable songs.

It wasn't about the money or the fame. Playing the piano while singing songs she'd penned about the pain that had ripped her heart in two alleviated those feelings. It seemed just as cathartic for audience members who sang along with tears in their eyes. That connection with her listeners meant everything.

That was what she wanted to share with the world.

Chase Stratton had name recognition and a string of hits under his belt. He took an artist's raw material and spun it into gold while respecting their unique sound.

She had something different to offer the world, and she needed a team around her discerning enough to recognize that.

She'd find another way to get to Chase. And when she did, she'd be ready.

Jessie grabbed a pen from her little side table, and the pile of magazines on it shifted. She picked up the ones that had fallen to the floor.

The financial magazine bore the image of the incredibly handsome Gideon Johns.

After all these years, sadness still swept over her whenever she thought of Gideon. And she hadn't been able to stop thinking of him since her recent return to Seattle for Matt Richmond's event. She'd been equal parts hopeful and terrified that she'd encounter Gideon for the first time in well over a decade.

Gideon had been the reason she'd written her very first song. A song of heartbreak and unrequited love. It had been one of the songs on the demo that earned Jessie her first songwriting gig with a small record company. So rather than resenting Gideon's rejection, she should thank him for breaking her heart.

Nothing had really happened between them back then. And nothing would happen between them in the future. So why couldn't she let thoughts of Gideon go?

Jessie tossed the magazines back onto the pile and returned to the piano, pen in hand.

She hated that she was still so affected by a man to whom she clearly hadn't meant anything. But berating herself over it wasn't productive. Instead, she would allow those frustrations to fuel her creativity so she could write the next song.

Jessie scribbled a few notes that had been playing in her head all day on the blank staff paper. Then she played the corresponding notes on her piano and started to sing.

Gideon Johns sat on the front edge of his large cherrywood desk. He folded his arms as he sized up his assistant, Landon Farmer. He had something to say, and whatever it was, he was fully aware that Gideon wasn't going to like it.

"Look, Landon, whatever it is you're dancing around here…just say it. We're both busy people."

"Our top two investors just pulled out of the United Arab Emirates deal." The words rushed out of his mouth.

"What?" Gideon's voice boomed, filling the room. He hadn't intended to shout, and since the man looked like he wanted to flee the room, he felt bad for doing so. Still, it was a natural reaction to discovering that he'd lost half of the capital he was counting on for a two-billion-dollar building project.

"What the hell happened? The last time I spoke with them, they were champing at the bit to get in on this deal. In fact, I didn't solicit either of them. They came to me."

"Both cited the recent volatility in their own industries, Mr. Johns." The man reverted to addressing him formally whenever Gideon was displeased.

"Do they have any idea how much I have riding on

this deal? This is our first project in Dubai. If word gets out that the deal is collapsing—"

"Then we don't let it collapse." Landon sat a bit straighter.

"And where do you propose we get nearly a billion dollars in the next two months?" Gideon raised an eyebrow.

"The company has considerable assets, sir. You already know that—"

"No." It was a single, nonnegotiable sentence.

"But, sir—"

"Investing in the project isn't an option." Gideon returned to his seat. His chest felt tight and his head was beginning to throb.

"But you just said what a disaster it would be if the project fails—"

"It won't fail. I'll find the money." Gideon looked at him pointedly.

"I have no doubt that you will, Mr. Johns." Landon straightened his tie. "But what if you can't secure the funds? Wouldn't it be better for our company to invest in the project than to have to admit we couldn't raise the capital?"

"Making real estate deals using other people's money has been my policy for the past ten years. If investors discover that I needed to liquidate assets and sink that kind of cash into my own project, it'll wreck the brand I've spent a decade building."

"We could do it discreetly," Landon suggested.

"I believe in being transparent with my investors."

Gideon frowned. "Besides, liquidating that kind of cash will inevitably attract attention."

"All valid points." Landon stood and massaged the nape of his neck. "I'll scour our database of potential investors and see who might be right for the Dubai project."

"Go for the big fish. And focus on those who have liquid assets readily available. We need to stick to our original timeline or the remaining investors will start to worry." Gideon made a mental note of the effects this sudden change might have on the project.

"There is one potential investor who comes to mind right away."

"I know." Gideon tapped the table. "Matt Richmond."

Matt was a friend who'd mused about investing in one of Gideon's projects, but had yet to pull the trigger.

Gideon made it a point not to pressure investors to join his projects. He simply laid out the opportunity and return on investment to be had, and allowed his track record and reputation to do the rest. The timing wasn't great, but he'd need to prod Matt and see if he was serious about investing.

This project had the potential to make all of them a shitload of money. He'd never take the project on if he didn't wholeheartedly believe that. Nor would he ever try to rope his friend, or any investor, into a shaky deal. But he needed to be a bit more direct with his friend.

"I've got Matt. I'll try to meet with him within

the next week." Gideon woke his computer screen to send an email to his friend. Another email captured his interest.

It was the Google alert he'd set up on singer/songwriter Jessie Humphrey. She was beautiful, brilliant, talented—and the little sister of his ex, Geneva Humphrey. The woman he'd planned to marry a lifetime ago. Right up until the moment she'd broken his heart.

He'd gotten over the break with Geneva. Had even come to realize she'd been right to end things between them. But his relationship with Jessie was more complicated.

Two years after his breakup with Geneva, Jessie had shown up at his door wanting more than just friendship.

She was his ex's sister, so he'd promptly sent her packing. But he hadn't ever been able to forget that day. Or get thoughts of Jessie out of his head.

The first time he heard Jessie Humphrey's voice flowing from the speakers of his Aston Martin Vanquish Volante he'd been over the moon with happiness for her.

She'd walked around wearing headphones and singing her heart out for as long as he'd known her. And despite her parents' insistence that she pursue a "real" career, Jessie had always wanted to share her gift with the world.

Now she was and he couldn't be more proud of her.

Gideon had carefully followed her career ever since.

"Is that all, boss?" Landon furrowed his brow.

"Yes, thank you." Gideon waited for the man to leave, closing the door behind him.

Gideon clicked the link in the email. It took him to a video of Jessie performing at a small club, seated at a piano.

She was stunning. Who knew that she'd turn into such a beautiful, confident young woman and a rising artist?

Jessie had such a powerful voice and a unique sound, even back when he'd known her. Geneva had teased Jessie about her incessant singing and starry-eyed dreams, but Gideon had loved to hear her sing. He'd told her that one day she'd be famous. And he'd been right.

When the performance ended, he listened to it twice more. Despite following Jessie's career, he'd decided against reaching out to her. After the way they'd left things, he doubted Jessie would welcome seeing him again. And he didn't need the heartbreak of falling for another Humphrey sister.

It was safer to admire Jessie from a distance.

Which was a shame, because he'd love to see her again.

Two

Teresa St. Claire had spent most of the week hiding out in her office. Once she arrived in the morning, she'd only peeked her head out when it had been absolutely necessary.

Yes, she was the boss. But she felt like the screwup employee who'd put the entire company in jeopardy.

Every time she closed her eyes, she could see the ugly headline that had been running for the past week.

Mogul's Torrid Affair with Father's Mistress Ends after Her Surprise Inheritance Revealed.

She'd been pegged as a home-wrecking gold digger who'd had an affair with the late Linus Christopher and now had her sights set on his heir Liam. The ugly rumors, complete with uncomplimentary videos and photos, lit up the airwaves and seemed to follow her everywhere online.

Teresa had been hounded by gossip columnists and bloggers. Even a woman she'd always considered a reputable reporter had shown up at her home, inquiring about the nature of Teresa's relationship with both Christopher men.

The effect the rumors were having on her business was bad enough. But the additional tension it had created between her and Liam was unbearable. She could only imagine the embarrassment the rumors were causing him.

Teresa wiped away warm tears when she recalled the expression on Liam's face when he'd confronted her about the rumors. He'd even had the audacity to imply that she might've been behind them. Still, her brain was flooded with the warmth and passion that had been growing steadily between them, despite his constant mistrust of her.

She sighed. The outer office was uncharacteristically quiet. Other than calls from gossip reporters, the phones barely rang. Her employees spoke in hushed tones with their heads together rather than with the jovial, energetic nature she was accustomed to.

At this rate, the doors of Limitless Events would be shuttered for good in a few weeks, and it would be her fault.

A knock at the door startled her from her thoughts.

Teresa sat ramrod straight in the chair behind her desk. "Come in."

Corinne, her personal assistant, stepped inside.

The woman dragged a hand through her headful of red corkscrew curls with an exasperated frown.

"We've had another cancellation, haven't we?" Teresa practically held her breath. That made three this week already. Not to mention the three or four clients who'd gotten nervous about having her plan their parties. It had been all she could do to calm them down so they wouldn't jump ship. But she realized that any one of them might change their minds at any time.

Corinne nodded. "Maggie Ellington called to say that she's sorry, but she just can't take a chance that the scandal won't have died down by the time of her daughter's wedding."

"That's understandable." Teresa tried to sound unaffected by the latest news. "She wants to make sure her daughter and son-in-law are the center of attention, not me."

"You mean she wants to make sure that *she's* the center of attention, and she won't be upstaged by anyone. Not even the bride." Corinne folded her arms.

"True." Teresa laughed and gave her assistant a reassuring smile. "But we'd both do the same if we were in her shoes. I can't blame her. In fact, I don't blame any of them for canceling."

"Well, I do." Corinne dropped into the chair in front of Teresa's desk. "They're all a bunch of hypocrites. Most of them have done more scandalous things on an average Tuesday than you're being accused of. Not to mention that the whole story is just a crock of—"

"I get it, Corinne." Teresa held up a hand to calm her assistant.

Corinne was fiercely loyal and feisty as hell. She knew how to get things done and she wasn't easily deterred. It made her an invaluable assistant. But it also meant that this situation wasn't sitting well with her.

"That may be true." Teresa shrugged. "But we can't force them to work with us."

"So what do we do in the meantime? The phones are barely ringing. If clients keep jumping ship…" Corinne's cheeks flushed.

"We won't let it get to that," Teresa said firmly. "I'm trying to drum up business with some new clients. The kind who don't run scared at the first hint of scandal."

"Reality stars?" Corinne asked, then rolled her eyes when Teresa confirmed with the nod of her head. "God, they're the worst." She heaved a sigh. "But hey, I get it. We have to do what we have to do. For now."

"The other key element of weathering this storm is that we hold on to as many current clients as we can. Keep reassuring them that this has all been a big misunderstanding and it'll blow over soon. Speaking of holding on to the clients we have now, have you heard from Matt Richmond?"

Limitless Events had planned an elaborate business retreat on behalf of Matt Richmond—the incredibly handsome and fabulously wealthy CEO of Richmond Industries—at The Opulence last week. The hotel was extravagant and luxurious, the food was going to be delectable, and the guest list was to include the rich and powerful. The event was the talk of the town, but for all the wrong reasons.

Torrential rains caused a mudslide that had knocked out the power and damaged the hotel before the retreat could take place. Matt Richmond's event should've been Limitless Event's pièce de résistance. Instead, it descended into a chaotic catastrophe for the dozen or so guests who'd arrived early. Though she obviously didn't control the weather, Teresa felt responsible for the calamitous party.

Thankfully, Matt Richmond hadn't blamed her for the disastrous nonevent. Undeterred by the incredible fail, he'd been determined to reschedule the retreat. Yet he hadn't called, as he'd promised, to initiate the planning.

Had he not returned her calls because of the scandal hitting the airwaves? Or had Liam, Matt's best friend, discouraged him from working with her?

"I haven't heard from him and whenever I've called, his assistant can't get a hold of him." Corinne shrugged apologetically. "Maybe we should call Nadia. After all, she does work for you."

"As an independent contractor," Teresa clarified. "And I don't like the idea of leveraging her marriage to Matt. That isn't why I asked her to work with me."

"Then maybe I should visit his office."

"No…don't." Teresa waved off the suggestion. She could imagine Corinne's friendly visit to Matt going wrong six ways to Sunday. "I'll try him again later. How is the search for a new venue going?"

Corinne's frown deepened and she blew a puff of air between her plump lips. "Not well. Not if Richmond is determined to schedule the retreat anytime soon. The venues with openings in the next couple of months don't meet our standards of elegance and luxury."

"I was afraid of that." Teresa heaved a sigh. "I know it's a tall order, but keep trying. Ask our top choices to call us first, in the event of a cancellation."

"Will do." Corinne popped up from her seat, her red curls bouncing. "Anything else, chief?"

"No." Teresa riffled through papers on her desk, knocking over a small four-by-six photo of her and her brother, Joshua, on a trip to Mexico together a few years ago. She picked up the photo. "Have you heard from my brother? He left me several messages when my phone went dead last week, but I haven't been able to contact him since then."

"I haven't taken any calls from him." Worry lined Corinne's forehead. "Should I try to raise him for you?"

"No, you have enough on your plate." Teresa set the photo back in place. "It's probably just Joshua being Joshua. I've left him several messages. He'll resurface when he's ready."

Corinne nodded, closing the door behind her.

Teresa relaxed in the comfy leather executive chair she'd splurged on when they'd opened the office. Now she only hoped she wouldn't be forced to shutter her doors and sell it along with everything else.

She was trying hard to keep it together, but it was a lot to ask when her entire world was imploding. The ill-fated weekend extravaganza, the false rumors, her brother's disappearance. But the thing that made her heart ache was Liam's rejection.

Amid the craziness of bad weather and a tree falling through the hotel that had nearly taken her out were moments that had taken her breath away. Her cheeks flushed and her entire body filled with heat whenever she thought of their steamy encounter in that spa room. And her heart stirred when she recalled the worry in his eyes when he'd rescued her from beneath that tree and tended to her ankle.

Without thought, Teresa rotated her ankle, still a little sore.

She'd been grateful he'd confided in her that night, explaining to her why he had such difficulty trusting people. But after all they'd been through and the moments they'd shared…how could he still not trust her?

Her desk phone rang and she picked it up. "Yes?"

"I tried Richmond's office again. His assistant was out and he answered," Corinne said triumphantly. "I have him on the line now."

Teresa smoothed a hand down her pant leg. "Thank you, Corinne. Please put him through."

"Hello, Matt, I know you're busy, so I'll only take a moment of your time," Teresa said cheerfully. "Last week, you indicated that you'd like to reschedule the retreat as soon as possible. I wanted to touch base so we can move forward with the plans."

There was a moment of uncomfortable silence. Teresa's pulse raced.

Oh no. He's going to cancel, too.

"When will The Opulence be available again?" he asked finally. "I know Shane Adams has people working around the clock, but…"

"Not anytime soon, I'm afraid. And once they do reopen, they're booked solid for several months. Would you like to wait until then?"

"No. It's for our fifth anniversary, so I'd like to keep the event as close to the anniversary date as possible. I realize not all of the people who were originally invited will be available if we reschedule with such a short timeline. So we'll need to expand the guest list based on how many from the original list will be able to attend."

"Just have your assistant pass those additional names on to Corinne and we'll take care of the rest."

"So then you have a venue in mind?" His tone was doubtful.

"Not yet," she admitted. "But my staff is working tirelessly to find a venue that's available on short notice and meets our standards and yours. I'll be in touch as soon as I have a few good options."

"And what about a headliner? Would Jessie Humphrey be willing to perform at the rescheduled event?"

Embroiled in a scandal and bleeding clients, Teresa hadn't considered whether Jessie would be willing to fly across the country again for the rescheduled event. Not to mention that she might have a conflict in her schedule.

"I'll do my very best to book her. Same deal?"

"Yes. I'll look forward to hearing from you once you've worked the details out."

Her phone pinged with a text message.

"I just sent you the two weekends that are most ideal for this event."

Teresa strained the panic from her voice. Both options were only a few weeks away. "I'll get right on it."

"Anything else?" he asked.

Teresa gripped the receiver tightly and nibbled her lower lip. She wanted desperately to ask Matt how his best friend was holding up under the glare of the rumors and innuendo about them. But this was business. Besides, she didn't want to drag Matt into this.

"No, but I wanted to say thank you for not giving up on my company or me despite everything that's happened. I can't tell you how much I appreciate it."

"You're welcome, Teresa," Matt said after a long pause. "Call me when you've got a venue and Jessie has confirmed."

Teresa hung up, grateful she still had Matt Richmond's confidence. She was more determined than ever to reward it.

"You can't just walk in there." She could hear Corinne's voice through the closed door.

Suddenly the door opened. Liam stood glaring at her.

"It's all right, Corinne." Teresa held up a hand. "I'll take it from here."

Corinne narrowed her eyes at him, then walked off in a huff.

"Have a seat." She gestured toward the chair when he closed the door behind him.

"I won't be staying long. I just came to remind you that, according to my father's will, your presence is required at Christopher Corporation's board meeting." He folded his arms.

His icy glare chilled her. He regarded her as if she were an untrustworthy stranger.

Had he forgotten that he'd shared his deepest vulnerabilities with her just a week ago? Brought her incredible pleasure on several occasions before that? Rescued her when she'd needed him desperately? They should be working together to clear their names, currently being dragged through the mud.

But the hardened look that distorted Liam's handsome face indicated that it would be a wasted argument. He was back to treating her as his enemy.

"In light of the rumors swirling about us, I didn't think you'd want me there." She raked her manicured fingernails through her shoulder-length blond hair.

"Pity my father's will didn't make allowances for bad press," he said dryly.

She folded her arms on the desk in front of her rather than raising the single digit that would best convey how she felt. "My assistant has access to my calendar. On your way out, stop by her desk and make an appointment."

Three

Liam's face and ears burned with heat in response to Teresa's brush-off. She'd summarily dismissed him and had returned her attention to the sheet of paper on her desk.

He clenched his jaw as he surveyed her. She was beautiful in a royal-blue silk blouse and white linen pantsuit. Teresa looked hurt and angry. She obviously just wanted him to be gone.

Liam couldn't blame her.

He'd blown into her office, behaving like an ass. But he was furious with her for putting his family and business in this position. *Again*. And he was furious with himself because he still wanted her...desperately. Despite everything that had happened. Despite the rumors swirling around about them. Despite the fact that he wasn't sure he could trust her.

Shit.

He must seriously be out of his mind because he wanted to trust her. And he cared for her. But he wouldn't allow anyone to make a fool of him. And there was still a strong possibility that was Teresa's endgame.

So why did he feel such a strong pull toward her? And why did he want her more than he'd ever wanted any woman?

Teresa insisted that her relationship with his late father had been strictly that of a mentor and his mentee. But the man he'd known his entire life would never have given a quarter of his company to anyone out of the mere goodness of his heart. Hell, he'd often wondered if Linus Christopher had possessed even an ounce of selflessness.

Was he really supposed to believe that the man who couldn't be bothered to show his own son warmth and compassion would've left this woman 25 percent of the company's shares unless there'd been something more to their relationship than either one of them had been willing to admit?

Teresa leaned back in her chair, narrowing her blue eyes at him. "Are you going to stand there all day brooding? This is my place of business. I have work to do."

Liam sighed. "Look, I know I came off like a complete ass just now. I'm sorry. But you need to face the fact that if you want to liquidate that stock, you'll need to comply with the stipulations of my father's will. That means we have to work together, and you need to be at the meeting this afternoon."

Teresa checked her calendar begrudgingly. "Fine. What time should I be there?"

"Actually, my car service is waiting. I thought we could ride over together so I could bring you up to speed on the meeting." Liam gestured toward the door.

"The sooner we leave, the sooner I can get back here." She pursed her lips in a sensual pout that made him want to take her in his arms and kiss her.

His hands balled into fists at his side.

She's the enemy. Why can't you remember that?

"It's best if we aren't seen leaving the building together," he mused aloud, more to himself than her.

"Then why are you here in my place of business? Or didn't you notice the stalkerazzi parked across the street?"

Liam straightened his tie. "I came in through the back entrance."

"Well, you can leave the same way you came in."

The hurt in her eyes and the pained tone of her voice made him feel as awful as his father. The last thing he wanted was to mimic Linus Christopher's cruelty. After his talk with Teresa, he'd thought a lot about his relationship with his father. And his relationship with her.

"If you need to bring me up to speed on the meeting, call me from your car. In fact, you could've done that in the first place rather than showing up here and *demanding* that I drop everything and come with you."

Liam squeezed the bridge of his nose. The situation was snowballing and he was the one to blame. "I'd like to go over a few documents in the car. It'll be much easier if we ride together in the limousine."

He shoved both his hands in his pockets and leaned against a tall wooden filing cabinet. Hoping she'd say yes. Because while every word he'd said about them needing to work together was true, the deeper truth was that he'd missed Teresa.

He missed the scent and feel of her skin, the way her sparkling blue eyes danced when she laughed and the sweet taste of her pouty lips. And he missed the incomparable ecstasy of watching Teresa St. Claire fall apart in his arms.

Teresa stood in the nude Stuart Weitzman block-heel sandals she'd worn in deference to her still-sore ankle. She retrieved her matching nude clutch from her desk drawer and walked to the door, only slightly favoring her injured leg.

"Your ankle…" He furrowed his brow. "Is it okay?"

"It's fine. Just a little sore." Teresa didn't want to think of Liam as the man who'd rushed to her rescue that night. Nor did she want to forget that he'd come charging into her office like an entitled ass who thought the world revolved around him. Still, she wouldn't behave like an ogre, even if he had. "Thank you again for what you did that night."

"I'm just glad you weren't seriously hurt. When

I think of what could've happened…" He seemed genuinely distressed by the near miss. "I'm just glad it didn't."

Don't be swayed by a few kind words.

She walked out to Corinne's desk, not acknowledging the evil eye her assistant was giving Liam.

"We're a go for the retreat." Teresa forwarded Matt's text to Corinne. "I just sent the dates Matt Richmond is interested in. Pull a couple of staff members in to call the entire guest list. Find out if either date is tenable. With such a short turnaround, we should get a feel for whether either date will work before we put too much time and effort into it."

"Got it." Corinne scribbled notes on a sheet of paper.

"I need a list of viable venues as soon as you can come up with them. I'll work on a few possibilities from my end, too. There has to be something available in Seattle that fits the bill for an event of this magnitude. Don't call Jessie Humphrey. I'll call her. A bit of persuading might be required after the nightmare we put her through last time."

Corinne nodded her agreement. She eyed Liam again, then shifted her gaze to Teresa. "Will you be returning to the office?"

Teresa cast a glance over her shoulder at Liam. He was especially handsome in a navy suit that hugged his strong frame and reminded her of all the reasons she loved the feel of his toned body pressed to hers.

But he'd rejected her after their unbelievably hot encounter at the spa. And again after the rumors about her being a scheming gold digger surfaced, despite the poignant moments they'd shared the night before.

Teresa's spine tensed. She gripped the clutch under her arm and reminded herself to hold on to that anger. So she'd never end up in Liam's bed again.

"I have every intention of returning here as soon as I can." Teresa turned and made her way toward the door, aware that every pair of eyes in the office was focused on her and Liam Christopher.

They left the building by the back entrance, where Liam's driver was waiting. Her cheeks stung at the thought of being shuttled away under cover because he was embarrassed to be seen with her. She slid across the leather seat, putting as much space as possible between them.

Liam had the audacity to look hurt.

"I know you have things you'd like to go over, but I need to make a call first. If there's any chance Jessie Humphrey isn't already obligated on the dates I have available, I don't want to miss my window of opportunity."

"Of course." He picked up a black leather portfolio and shuffled through its contents.

Teresa pulled up Jessie Humphrey's number and hoped things would finally go her way.

Four

Jessie closed her eyes and settled into eagle pose, her left leg wound around her right and her right arm wrapped around her left. Unable to keep her mind still long enough to formally meditate, she enjoyed the moving meditation of yoga.

The ring of her cell phone disturbed her peaceful solitude.

She unraveled her arms and legs and peeked at the caller ID.

"Teresa St. Claire." She muttered the name under her breath, then considered ignoring it until she'd finished her yoga practice.

But Teresa had indicated that Matt Richmond wanted to reschedule his event. Despite the chaos of the heavy rains, power outage, and a tree falling into the hotel which nearly took Teresa out... Matt Richmond had generously paid her the full agreed-upon amount of her contract without quibbling.

If she was going to do this project independently, without the backing of her label or the blessing of her agent, she needed an infusion of cold, hard cash.

Jessie answered the call just before it went to voice mail. "Hello."

"Jessie, it's Teresa. I'm glad I caught you. Matt Richmond has decided to reschedule his retreat. The only bright spot to the entire ordeal at The Opulence was your impromptu concert in the lobby. I swear, it's probably the only thing that kept the guests from rioting." Teresa's words were rushed and her voice seemed tense. "So, of course, he'd like you to per-form at the rescheduled event."

Not wanting to sound too eager, Jessie hesitated before responding. "That's nice of you to say, Teresa. The situation got pretty intense, so I'm glad I was able to help. The event isn't going to be held there again, is it? It was a lovely hotel, but after the mud-slide I'm not in love with hotels situated on a cliff."

"Understood. It'll be a while before The Opulence is up and running again anyway. And Matt would really like to get this retreat done soon—"

"How soon?"

"He's considering two weekends this month." Teresa's tone was tentative. "I'm hoping you'll be available on one of them."

Jessie grimaced. She'd planned to spend the month writing songs for her next album and securing the producers and musicians she wanted to work with on her dream project. "Actually, I cleared my calendar to work on my next album."

"I can appreciate how busy you must be, Jessie, but if you have any flexibility at all, you know Matt Richmond will make it worth your while. We'd do the same generous deal as last time. In addition to your booking fee, we'll pay for your flight via private jet, and all of your room service expenses at the hotel."

Jessie chewed on her lower lip and paced the floor. "I don't know. This album is really important to me. I didn't tell you before, but I've decided not to re-sign with my current label. I plan to start my own, so I'll have the freedom to make songs like the ones I performed that day in the lobby."

"I applaud your decision, Jessie. I did the same when I broke away from MSM Events and started my own company. So I know how rewarding it can be, but I also know that you need money and connections when you're breaking out on your own. And at Richmond Industries' fifth anniversary gala, you'll have an opportunity to nab both."

"What do you mean?" Jessie sat on the edge of her sofa. "Who's going to be at the retreat?"

"Since not all of the invited guests will be able to attend on such short notice, Matt instructed me to expand the list. If there's a producer or music exec you're eyeing for your new project, I could try to have them added to the guest list. I can't promise you

they'll attend, but I'll do my best to get them there.
I'll even seat you at the same table."

Jessie sat on the piano bench. As much as she'd
like to spend the next several weeks immersed in
this project, if she was going to make it a reality,
she needed the money she'd get from this gig. And if
Teresa St. Claire could get her at a table with Chase
Stratton or Dixon Benedict and allow her to showcase some of the new material she was working on
for the album, all the better.

"And if you're looking for wealthy music lovers
who might be willing to help bankroll your project,
there'll be a few in attendance, I'm sure. Also, we
might be able to increase your exposure by broadcasting your performance live this time. If that's
something you want, I'll talk to Nicolette Ryan about
it."

There were too many benefits to this deal to ignore. "You've got a deal. Send the contract over to
my agent."

Sinking onto the mat, Jessie tried to resume her
yoga practice.

She'd managed to avoid Gideon Johns the last
time she'd returned to Seattle. Maybe she could
again. The money and exposure were worth the risk.

If she did cross paths with him, things didn't need
to be awkward. She couldn't stop thinking of him,
but he probably hadn't given her another thought.
So she'd hold her head high, greet him politely and
move on with her life.

Jessie allowed her eyes to drift closed as she inhaled a deep breath. Everything would be fine. In fact, it might be good to see Gideon again. Perhaps it would prompt her to relinquish the silly fantasy she still held on to. Then she could finally let go of the past and any thoughts of what might've been.

"Good news." Landon knocked on the partially open door of Gideon's office. "You won't have to pin Matt Richmond down for a meeting after all."

"Why not?" Gideon looked up from his laptop where he'd been writing an email, trying to close the deal with a potential investor in the Dubai project. "Have we gotten all the capital we need?"

"Not yet." Landon frowned as he took a few steps inside Gideon's office. "But we're close. And I think we might've gotten even closer. I just confirmed that you'll be available to attend the rescheduled Richmond Industries anniversary retreat."

Gideon leaned back in his seat and rubbed his chin. "Matt is hosting the event, so it'll be hard to pin him down for a one-on-one presentation."

"I'll put together a quick video presentation with all of the basic facts. Something eye-catching that'll grab his attention." Landon slid into the chair in front of Gideon's desk. "You can hand him a copy of the prospectus as well as email it to him so he can review it at length."

"Good work, Landon."

"Thanks." He grinned, settling in the chair.

Gideon raised an eyebrow. "Guess that means you'd better get to work."

"Right." Landon hopped up quickly and headed for the door. "Oh, and I sent you over that list of prospective investors."

"I'm working on it now," Gideon confirmed. He peered through his thumb and forefinger. "I'm this close to securing another hundred million."

Landon's phone rang. But rather than a traditional ringer, it played a familiar song.

"That song…"

"Sorry, I usually turn my ringer off in the office, but I just came back from lunch and—"

"That's a Jessie Humphrey song, isn't it?" He'd recognize Jessie's soulful, heart-wrenching voice anywhere.

"Yeah, it's one of the more obscure songs on her recent album. It doesn't get any radio play, but if you ask me, it's one of the best songs on the album." Landon seemed impressed that he knew who Jessie Humphrey was. "My girlfriend loves the song, too. That's why I chose it as her ringtone."

"Well, you'd better call her back, huh?" Gideon went back to typing out his email.

"Right. But I'll send you the tentative dates for the retreat first. And I'll get to work on that presentation just as soon as I can."

Gideon hit Send on the email. Then he pulled out his phone and searched for Jessie's recent album. He'd purchased every album she'd made and the songs she wrote for other artists over the years.

Despite the debacle of the kiss, Jessie had been a

friend. Someone he truly cared for. He wanted only the best for her.

He stared at the album cover where Jessie sat in a leather chair wearing a short, flirty dress and a sexy smile. He often wondered if things would've turned out differently between them if more time had passed after his breakup with Geneva before Jessie had kissed him. Would he still have reacted negatively? Or would he have kissed her back?

Gideon shook the thought from his brain. They'd both gone on to fulfill their dreams. Wasn't that proof enough that things had happened just as they should?

He scrolled through the song list. Most of the songs on this album had an upbeat pop sound. But the song Landon had chosen as his girlfriend's ringtone was more like the soulful performance Jessie had given in that intimate little club. It was the kind of song that made her unique vocals shine.

Gideon shut the door to his office and played the song on repeat, losing himself in the mellow sound of Jessie's voice and her heartbreaking lyrics.

Five

Teresa ended the call with Jessie Humphrey, holding back a squeal of glee. In an otherwise crappy day, this was a victory worth celebrating.

She tapped out a quick email to Corinne confirming that Jessie Humphrey would perform. She asked her assistant to make sure the contract was ready to send the moment they selected a date and secured the venue.

Teresa checked the shared spreadsheet updating which guests were available on either of the possible weekends.

"Shit," Teresa mumbled under her breath.

"What's wrong?" Liam stopped scanning the documents in his folder. His smoldering blue eyes seemed to slice right through her. "You just secured your headliner. I'd think you'd be ecstatic."

"I'm thrilled that Jessie confirmed." Teresa ignored the fluttering in her belly and the electricity that danced along her spine when he stared at her that way. "But I'm not happy that most of the guests are selecting the earlier date. That gives us just two weeks to find a venue and get everything in motion. So far, every suitable venue in Seattle is booked. I'm going to have to venture outside the area."

"Have you considered Napa Valley?" Liam returned his attention to the documents.

"That's at least six hundred miles from Seattle."

"Seven, but who's counting?" Liam's eyes danced when they met hers and a sexy little smirk curved one corner of his mouth. It reminded her of the look he'd given her when he'd...

Teresa shut her eyes and tried to push thoughts of their amazing nights together from her brain.

"That would considerably increase the cost of the event."

"True. But it might also lure more people there. Especially those who are still unhappy about what happened at the previous event in Seattle. The beauty of the vineyards and an endless supply of wine will earn you a lot of forgiveness with this crowd. Besides, it's the company's fifth anniversary. Matt needs to make a big splash with this event so everyone will forget what happened at The Opulence."

"All good points, but I can't book a venue without seeing it for myself. I need to make sure there's adequate event space, suitable accommodations and trained, professional staff. I'd need to sample the food and attest to the cleanliness of the rooms. I'd want to talk to people who've used the venue before to make sure their level of customer service is on par with what my clients expect."

"So find a few possible venues and fly there and check them out." Liam shrugged.

Teresa gritted her teeth. Was he being intentionally flippant about something that could make or break her?

"I would, but my private plane is in the shop." She dropped her phone in her clutch and snapped it shut.

Liam chuckled, his eyes twinkling. "Then by all means, take mine."

"Now you're just being cruel." She folded her arms and pursed her lips. "I know this doesn't mean anything to you, but this event is important to me. With everything that's going on right now, this might be my only chance to keep my company from going under."

"I wasn't being facetious." His tone and expression seemed genuinely apologetic. "I'm being sincere."

Teresa stared at him, blinking. "I don't get it. Not an hour ago you could barely stand to be in the same room with me. Now you're offering to let me use your private plane to plan your friend's event?"

"That's just it," he said quickly. "Matt's my best friend and this event is important to him. I want to ensure his retreat succeeds. Besides, Matt and I will be making the announcement about our joint venture, the Sasha Project, so I'm invested in the success of this event, too. That's why I'd like to accompany you on this scouting trip."

Teresa stared at him blankly, still waiting for him to pull the rug from beneath her. She sifted her fingers through her hair. "I'll have to check with Matt first. If he's good with relocating the event to Napa Valley, I'll gladly accept your offer. Thank you."

"Anything for a friend," Liam said calmly, though his heart danced in his chest. He could barely keep from smiling at the thought of spending time alone with Teresa in Napa Valley.

She's supposed to be the enemy.

Yet he wanted to haul her onto his lap and kiss her like it was the only kiss he'd ever need. The way he'd kissed her when last she'd been in his arms.

His eyes drifted to her momentarily, scanning the royal-blue silk blouse that was a welcome pop of color against her stark white linen pantsuit.

Teresa always managed to look so buttoned up and proper. It was a calm facade that gave no indication of the raging heat and unbridled passion that lay beneath her cool exterior.

Liam's face and chest flushed with heat and his heart thumped so hard in his chest he wondered if she could hear it, too.

Being in such close proximity to Teresa made it difficult to remain aloof and pretend he didn't want her as much now as he ever had. That he didn't think of her constantly.

It would be a painfully long twelve months.

According to his father's will, that was how long Teresa had to take a role in the company before she could divest herself of the shares he'd left her. That meant twelve months of working closely while rumors swirled around them and this palpable heat raged between them.

He honestly didn't know if he could take it.

Teresa had been tapping out a text message on her phone, presumably floating the idea of moving the event to Napa Valley past Matt.

"There." She put her phone on the seat between them. "We'll see what he says."

"Great. Now about this meeting." He handed a portfolio to her. "Here's the basic information you'll need to know this afternoon. We'll be meeting with the board to—"

Teresa's phone dinged and she picked it up. She grinned, turning the screen toward him. "Matt loves the idea. Now I just hope I can find a venue for our preferred date."

Liam flipped his wrist and looked at his watch. It was clear Teresa wouldn't be able to focus on anything else until she had some peace of mind about finding a venue.

Liam placed a call to his assistant.

"Duncan, please email Teresa St. Claire our list of preferred hotel venues in Napa Valley. Preferably those near a vineyard. And be sure to copy her assistant Corinne on it. Thanks."

Liam ended the call and put his phone away. "Let Corinne know she should call off the search for Seattle venues. Then maybe we can get to the business at hand."

Teresa stared at him. "Why would you—?"

"Same reason. I'm doing this for Matt and for myself. I need you to focus on Christopher Corporation right now, and until that was resolved, it was apparent you wouldn't be able to."

He opened his portfolio after she'd sent her text message. "Now let's get started."

Six

Gideon had been working in his office all morning with the door closed and Jessie's first album playing. She'd hit the music charts with one or two of the songs from her most recent album. But the songs on this older EP were far better. Her voice had a raw edge that reminded him of Alicia Keys's first album. And the songs all seemed so personal and heartrending.

He couldn't help thinking of her older sister Geneva and how heartsick he'd been when she'd broken it off with him. But he was also reminded of the day two years later when Jessie had shown up at his place.

Gideon couldn't help cringing at the memory.

He didn't regret rejecting Jessie's advances then.

It was the right thing to do. But he did regret *how* he'd handled the encounter. He would never forget the heartbreak and pain in those dark brown eyes. It haunted him still.

Gideon paused as he listened to the song.

"I was so young. Did you have to be so cruel? All I ever really wanted was you."

He rubbed his jaw.

Was the song about their encounter that day?

Maybe it made him arrogant to speculate whether the incident between him and Jessie had been the inspiration for the song. But it'd been fifteen years, and he hadn't been able to get that day out of his mind. Was it really so implausible that it'd had a lasting impact on her, too?

Gideon massaged the base of his skull, where tension always gathered.

The Humphrey sisters.

Painful memories of both Geneva and Jessie were inextricable parts of his past. As were the happy memories of them that he'd always treasure. So he could never regret the rainy Saturday afternoon he'd first encountered the pair at a local movie theater. Or the ways in which that encounter had shaped his life.

As painful as it'd been, the dissolution of his relationship with Geneva had been the best thing for both of them. He wouldn't be the man he was today if not for his drive to prove Geneva and her snobby, elitist parents wrong.

It had taken a while for him to get over the sting of

her rejection, but Gideon harbored no regrets about Geneva. But Jessie... He groaned.

Jessie was another matter altogether.

He'd considered contacting her, if for no other reason than to apologize for handling the situation so badly. But he'd decided against it.

He would welcome the chance to make peace with Jessie. But he wouldn't reopen an old wound just to absolve himself of guilt.

There was no point in revisiting old hurts. What was done was done.

So despite his desire to make it up to Jessie for hurting her, some relationships were better left in the past.

Seven

Liam lagged a bit behind Teresa and Evelyn Montague, the manager of The Goblet Hotel and Vineyards in Napa Valley, as the woman offered them a tour of the facility.

The vineyards and the grounds of the hotel were lovely. The hotel itself had loads of charm, something he knew both Matt and Teresa would appreciate. The art deco style hotel featured lots of chrome, silver, black and red. The furniture and wallpaper sported bold geometric shapes. The lighting, the mirrors, and much of the furniture and finishes exuded an iconic elegance of days past. Yet the hotel was tastefully modern and chic. The Goblet offered style and luxury without being pretentious.

It was the reason he'd fallen in love with the place when he'd visited it several years ago.

"I can't believe that you can accommodate our event on such short notice. A hotel this beautiful... I was sure you'd be booked." Teresa's eyes roamed the sumptuous space as they entered one of the ballrooms.

"Yes, well..." Evelyn glanced back at him, then cleared her throat. "We had some cancellations."

"I'm sorry to hear that." Teresa stared at the woman, following her gaze. She looked at Liam quizzically, the wheels turning in that pretty head of hers. She returned her gaze to Evelyn. "But it certainly worked out to my advantage, for which I'm appreciative."

Her thank-you seemed to be addressed to both him and Evelyn.

Teresa flipped her blond hair over her shoulder and straightened her suit jacket. "I've seen all I need to see. I'm prepared to sign the paperwork as soon as it's ready."

"Very good." Evelyn nodded. "I have a couple of items to handle first. So please, enjoy lunch and cocktails on the house. The covered patio overlooking the vineyard is quite lovely."

"That would be wonderful. Thank you." Teresa's blue eyes glinted in the sunlight spilling through the windows.

They followed the woman to the dining space, then she whispered something to their server before excusing herself.

There was an awkward lull of silence between them as they reviewed their menus. Finally, Teresa spoke.

"I honestly can't thank you enough, Liam."

"For?" He raised a brow, still surveying his menu. The offerings had changed since last he was there.

"For recommending Napa Valley and The Goblet." She put her menu down and leaned forward. "More importantly, thank you for whatever you did to convince them to make space for our event."

"Me?" He feigned ignorance.

"Please don't pretend you don't know what I'm talking about. I saw the look Evelyn exchanged with you. There was no cancellation, was there?"

Liam put his menu down and straightened his tie without response. He avoided her mesmerizing blue eyes, for fear his would reveal anything more.

He said instead, "What looks good to you?"

You.

Teresa bit back the automatic response perched on the edge of her tongue.

He was wearing a lightweight gray gabardine suit that fit him to perfection. His baby-blue shirt nicely complemented the icy blue eyes that calmly assessed her.

"You didn't answer my question." She sipped her water. "You must've gone to a lot of trouble to make this happen. As grateful as I am for what you've done, I'm completely perplexed. Why would you go to such lengths to help me?"

"Matt's my best friend, and I try to help my friends whenever I can. They'd do the same for me."

"You're a bit of a fixer yourself."

Liam chuckled. "Never thought of it that way before."

She hadn't heard the sound of his laugh in so long. It was nice to hear it again.

"Well, even if you did this for Matt, I want you to know how much I appreciate it. With everything that's been going on lately…" Her shoulders tensed as the weight of the rumors and lost business settled on her again. "Limitless Events won't survive if I don't pull this off. So thank you."

"You're welcome." He furrowed his brow. "And I'm sorry I accused you of leaking information about us to the media. Someone is obviously trying to damage your business and reputation."

"Do you have any idea who might've done it? Not many people knew about us. And I don't believe any of them would ever do something like this."

"Isn't it more likely it was one of the reporters you invited to your events?"

"Are you suggesting this is my fault because I invited the media?"

"No. But you can't blame me for being wary of them until we get to the bottom of this."

That she could understand.

What she couldn't understand was why Liam insisted on accompanying her on the trip and touring the hotel with her.

Did he really expect her to believe he'd done all

of that because he and Matt were best friends or be-cause of their collaboration on the Sasha Project?

"Are you sure it's a good idea for us to stay over-night at the same hotel with all of the rumors already out there about us?" She glanced at the server, who seemed to be staring at them whenever she looked up.

"We're both part of Christopher Corporation for now. This is a working trip. Duncan is still trying to get me an early-morning meeting with the CEO of a local medical technology company I've been eyeing. It'd make an excellent acquisition for our portfolio, but the owner isn't very enthusiastic about the possibility."

"I didn't realize Christopher Corporation dabbled in the medical field."

"Our interests are quite diverse. Real estate, tech-nology, entertainment…any solid investment that piques my interest and will provide a good return.

"If you'd read the company material I had sent over, you'd know this."

She ignored the jab. "So maybe this medical tech company just isn't interested in selling."

"I have it on good authority they are. I get the sense they just don't want to sell to me."

Liam thanked the sommelier when he brought out the bottle of four-year-old cabernet sauvignon Evelyn had recommended and decanted it. Then the server brought their appetizers. Artisanal cheeses with a charcuterie tray and crackers, both house-made.

"Why wouldn't they want to sell to you?" Teresa

sipped her cabernet. The savory, full-bodied liquid, bursting with the flavor of plums and berries, rolled over her tongue.

Liam's cheeks and forehead flushed as he studied her intently. He loosened his tie. "I'd say it has everything to do with the kind of person my father was."

"Linus shouldn't be an issue for them anymore." Teresa hoped she didn't sound insensitive.

"The culture and philosophy of a company often survive its founder. Especially when a family member takes over." Liam swirled the dark liquid in his glass, then took a sip. "They probably suspect I'll run the company the same way."

"Show them that isn't true." Teresa piled duck prosciutto and Fourme d'Ambert onto a cracker and took a bite. "Oh my God. That's good," she muttered, one hand shielding her full mouth.

Liam's eyes darkened and his Adam's apple bobbed as he swallowed hard. He spread duck rillettes and a savory goat cheese on a toasted baguette. "If they'd returned any of the calls Duncan made to them, I'd happily reassure them I'm nothing like my father."

She took another sip of wine and spread foie gras on a cracker. "Call the CEO yourself and request an informal meeting. Don't dance around the issue. Go at it head-on. Let him know that while you respected your father, you didn't always agree with his methods. You have a different vision for Christopher Corporation. One you'd like his company to have a starring role in."

Liam rubbed his chin, his head tilted thoughtfully. "My father might've been an asshole, but people respected him. I can't go into this deal with him thinking we're coming from a weakened position."

"Sometimes a softer touch makes a stronger impact. Besides, it'll give you a common enemy and a chance to bond because of it."

Liam put prosciutto on a cracker and popped it into his mouth.

"What I've been doing clearly isn't working," he conceded. "Maybe it's time to try something new."

"To new beginnings, then." She lifted her glass.

"To new beginnings." Liam clinked his glass against hers.

They both seemed to relax into an easy, comfortable conversation that reminded her of the nights they'd spent talking and making love. Before the will was revealed. Before those rumors had started flying, wrecking the fragile relationship they'd been building.

Teresa's mind whirred with unsettling thoughts. About her turbulent, off-and-on relationship with Liam. Her unpredictable brother, who still hadn't returned any of her calls. The rumors that were causing her to hemorrhage clients and whoever might be behind them.

"Teresa." Liam's large, warm hand covered hers. "Is everything all right?"

She glanced down at his hand and he quickly withdrew it, pressing it to the table.

"Yes, of course." She bit back the tears that burned her eyes. "I'm fine."

She most definitely was *not* fine.

Teresa was angry. With Liam for the distance he'd put between them when she was given shares of Christopher Corporation. With whoever leaked those ridiculous affair rumors to the press. But most of all, she was angry with herself. Because despite it all, she couldn't help still wanting him.

She longed for the heat that had raged between them during their past toe-curling encounters. But she also longed for the tenderness in his touch the night he'd rescued her from beneath that fallen tree. And the vulnerability he'd displayed later that night when he'd told her about the awful relationship he'd had with his parents.

Teresa drew in a deep breath. It was nice enjoying a delicious meal and incredible wine with Liam as they overlooked the vineyard, with no qualms about who might see them. But it was the exception, not the rule. So she shouldn't read anything into it or expect it again. She should just enjoy it.

She needed to get through the next year quietly, without any more incidents or negative press.

Liam's phone buzzed for the third time. He glanced at his watch. "I can't believe we've been here three hours." He'd forgotten how easy she was to talk to.

"No wonder the staff has been circling us." Her eyes gleamed.

Liam couldn't pull his gaze from her bright smile.

Teresa was beautiful, but there was something much deeper that appealed to him. She was smart and diligent, and she seemed so sincere.

He wanted to believe her interest in him wasn't a calculated ploy to grab a bigger piece of Christopher Corporation. That she genuinely enjoyed his company as much as he enjoyed hers.

"Is everything okay?" She regarded him with concern, her head tilted. "Do you need to take that call?"

"It's nothing pressing." Liam slid his phone into the pocket inside his suit jacket.

Teresa put her phone back in her purse and indicated to the server that they were finally ready to leave. She returned her attention to Liam. "Thank you again. You didn't have to do any of this, but I'm glad you did." She smiled. "Despite all of your posturing, you're a really good guy."

His heart swelled, but then it was seized by guilt over having accused her of running a scheme on his family.

"Let's make that our little secret. Don't want the competition thinking I've gone soft." He winked at her and then left some cash on the table for the server.

They'd spent three hours talking about the mundane. From Matt and Nadia's wedding to how Seattle's sports teams were doing this year. Over a second bottle of cabernet sauvignon, they discussed which Netflix shows were worth binge-watching.

All safe topics.

The server smiled broadly when he spied the additional tip Liam had left on the table. "Can I get you two anything else? A dessert perhaps? I can have it sent to your room."

"*Rooms*," Teresa clarified. "We're work associates."

The way the man's eyes danced made it clear he believed otherwise. "Shall I have something sent to your rooms?" He stressed the *s* at the end of the word. "On the house, too, of course."

"I couldn't eat another bite…until dinner." Teresa rubbed her belly. "But please give our compliments to the chef. The food was spectacular and your service was impeccable."

The man thanked them, then stepped aside, allowing them to exit the table.

When Teresa stood, she teetered slightly. Liam placed his hands on her waist to steady her. Their eyes met for a moment.

"That cabernet sneaks up on you." She pressed a hand to her forehead. "I'd better lie down before dinner."

"I'll walk you to your room." Liam guided her toward the exit, his hand resting on the small of her back. The server gave him a knowing grin.

Just great.

The server didn't believe they were simply business associates and Liam was to blame.

Accompanying Teresa on this trip was a bad idea. Suggesting they stay overnight was an even worse one.

They were in Napa Valley, rather than in Seattle where the rumors about them were swirling. He hoped they'd be safe here. He'd always been impressed by how discreet and respectful of his privacy the staff at The Goblet had been. He had no reason to suspect that this time would be different.

As they rode the elevator up to her room, his hand grazed hers. A rush of pleasure flooded his senses as he recalled the sensation of her soft, bare skin caressing his when last he'd held her in his arms.

He tried to block out the growing desire to back her against the elevator wall and claim her sweet mouth in a demanding kiss. Graze her nipples with his thumbs through the silky material.

Suddenly, the elevator chimed, indicating they'd arrived on her floor.

She exited the elevator. "Will I see you for dinner?"

"I'll walk you to your door." He stepped off, too. She'd seemed slightly tipsy, so he wouldn't rest unless he knew Teresa was safely in her room.

She seemed pleased by his offer.

"Dinner would be nice. I'll pick you up at your door around seven."

"Or I could meet you downstairs."

"It's like you said… I'm a nicer guy than I let on."

They stopped in front of her door and she opened it, stepping inside.

"Thank you again, Liam. The hotel is perfect for Matt's retreat. You have no idea how badly I needed this win." Her lips quirked in a soft, dreamy smile that lit her beautiful eyes. "This has been a really lovely day. After all of the crappy ones I've had this past week, I needed a day like this. So thank you." She looked at him expectantly.

Liam leaned against the doorway, his arms folded as he stood just over the threshold from Teresa. There was barely a foot of space between them. He wanted to lean in, erase the distance between them and take her in his arms. Kiss her until they were both breathless.

The eager look in her eyes and the soft pout of her kissable lips indicated it was what she wanted, too. But he'd promised himself he'd stay strong, so they wouldn't end up tumbling into bed.

There was too much unresolved baggage between them. So as wonderful as the good times they'd shared were, those moments where overshadowed by the pain, distrust and resentment that still bubbled just beneath the surface for both of them.

Liam heaved a long sigh as he pushed off the wall. "I'm going to give that CEO a call, like you suggested. Thank you for a lovely afternoon."

Liam strode toward the waiting elevator before he changed his mind.

Eight

Jessie put down her pen and huffed. She'd written two new songs for her album, but she was still struggling to write the title song. The one that would stand as a metaphor for her ability to rebound from both heartbreak and the disappointment in her mentor, Arnold Diesman, the record label's top exec, turning out to be a lecherous jerk.

She unrolled her yoga mat, sucked in a deep breath and went into her favorite sun salutation. It was the perfect way to alleviate the stress she was feeling, and it got her creative juices flowing.

Jessie bent over into a deep forward fold, her hands pressed to the mat and the blood rushing to her brain.

Her phone rang.

Figures.

Her phone had been silent all day, but the moment she'd gone into moving meditation, not wanting to be disturbed, it rang.

She checked the screen. *Teresa St. Claire.*

Jessie answered. "Hi, Teresa. What's up?"

"Hi, Jessie. Great news. We've nailed down the date and venue. The retreat happens in two weeks and you're going to adore the venue. It's a cute little art deco boutique hotel and vineyard in Napa Valley. I'm here now. The place is incredible. Very Old Hollywood glamour." The woman spoke excitedly.

"Didn't want to take another chance on Seattle rain and calamitous mudslides, huh?" Jessie wasn't sure if she was more relieved by not having to deal with the dreary weather or avoiding an encounter with Gideon.

She'd frittered away too much of the time she should've spent writing this album with imagining what it would be like to see Gideon again.

"With the short notice, we just couldn't find another venue in Seattle that was both available and luxurious enough for this event." Teresa's response brought Jessie out of her temporary, Gideon-induced haze. "Otherwise, I would've loved to keep the event in Seattle where most of the guests are based."

Lucky me.

"I've always wanted to go to Napa Valley, so I'm looking forward to it." Jessie sat on the piano bench with her back to the keys. "Send the updated contract with all of the particulars to my agent. We'll get it executed and return it as soon as possible."

"Corinne will send the contract first thing in the morning," Teresa said. "And more good news... Matt Richmond approved adding Chase Stratton and Dixon Benedict to the guest list. He was thrilled you suggested them. Both men were on his radar for future projects. He'll invite them both personally tomorrow. I can't confirm yet that either man will be there, but as promised, they'll both be invited."

"Keep me posted on whether they RSVP?"

"I will, and one more thing." Jessie could hear the grin in Teresa's voice. "I told you that wealthy music lovers who might invest in your indie project would be in attendance. Well, I'm reviewing the updated guest list and I just got confirmation that real estate billionaire Gideon Johns will be there as well as—"

"Gideon Johns RSVP'd?" Jessie began pacing the floor, her heart racing. She'd managed to avoid Gideon when the Seattle retreat was canceled. She obviously wouldn't have the same luck in Napa.

"Yes, and I'd be happy to introduce you."

"That won't be necessary," Jessie responded tersely. "We've met."

"I see." Teresa's voice registered worry. She was silent for a moment, then asked tentatively. "Gideon's presence won't be a problem for you, will it?"

Part of her was eager to show Gideon that the girl he'd dismissed was now an in-demand recording artist. But another part of her dreaded the encounter. A man as rich and powerful as Gideon probably barely remembered her, while she'd thought of him often over the years.

But she wouldn't allow the possibility to sidetrack her career. Nor did she need Gideon's help.

"No." Jessie forced herself to smile. "He's my older sister's ex-boyfriend, that's all. He probably doesn't even remember me. Thank you for the call. I'll look for the contract from my agent."

Jessie ended the call and continued to pace the floor.

Why should she care whether Gideon would be at the retreat? She should be over what happened between them fifteen years ago and over him. But her mind was buzzing with memories of the man who'd wanted to marry her sister.

The man she'd had a killer crush on from the first time she'd laid eyes on him when she and her older sister Geneva met him one Saturday afternoon at the movie theater.

Their parents hadn't been thrilled about Geneva getting serious with a poor kid from the wrong side of the tracks. But the more they objected, the more Geneva dug in.

Her sister had truly cared for Gideon, in the beginning. But at some point, it became more about defying their parents than genuine affection for him.

On her sister's birthday, Gideon had presented Geneva with an engagement ring. That's when her sister realized she'd let things go too far.

Geneva was about to embark on a year of traveling

in Europe and she wanted the freedom to see other people. So she'd kissed Gideon tenderly and ended it.

Gideon had been devastated, and so was Jessie.

She'd adored him.

Jessie sat on her yoga mat, her legs folded in lotus position. Eyes squeezed shut, she inhaled a deep breath, trying to shut out the heartbreak she'd experienced the day she'd told Gideon how she really felt about him. But as a songwriter, she was in an unenviable position.

She needed to conjure up the raw emotions she'd felt that day. Feelings that compelled her to pen songs about unrequited love, living through the pain of a shattered heart and learning to rebuild it. How else could she convey that pain so palpably that the audience felt it, too?

But that meant that in moments like this, her wounded heart bled afresh. As if it had happened yesterday instead of a decade and a half ago.

She certainly hadn't spent her entire adult life pining away for Gideon. But in moments like this, it was clear she'd never really gotten over him.

"Gideon, we need to talk." Landon stood in the doorway of Gideon's office looking flustered.

The kid was brilliant, but Gideon wondered if he'd ever have the steely spine it took to deal with the ups and downs of real estate.

Financial and real estate journals had proclaimed that Gideon had the Midas touch. But he never fell for his own hype. He was good at the real estate game and had a gut sense of what deals and which investors were right for a project. But nothing was foolproof.

Gideon nodded toward the seat in front of his desk and leaned back in his executive chair. "What's happened now?"

"Some of the smaller investors in the Dubai deal are nervous because they've learned that our two largest investors pulled out of the deal. No one has jumped ship yet, but I get the sense they're considering it."

"You did the preliminary work on this deal. Are you confident in your research?"

"Yes, of course. I did solid background on everyone involved. I've run comps in the region. It's a hot area. Demand for and the price of hotel rooms continues to climb. New shops and restaurants are going up. Investors from around the world are clamoring to get in on deals in the area." Landon spoke animatedly. He seemed insulted by the insinuation that the preparatory work he'd done was lacking.

"*That* level of confidence…" Gideon pointed to the younger man. "That's what you need to convey to any investor who might be getting cold feet. They wanted to be part of this deal and they understood the inherent risks. So what they really want to hear is that *we're* still completely on board with the deal."

Landon nodded thoughtfully. "I can do that."

"Next time one of them calls, let them hear the fire and bass in your voice that I just heard."

"You can count on me." Landon was infinitely

more self-assured than he'd been when he entered the room. "One other thing…we have a limited window of time here. We'll all feel more confident about the deal once the remaining funding has been secured. I know you have meetings lined up with several potential investors, but Matt Richmond isn't among them."

Gideon had hoped to bring up the deal in casual conversation with his friend. But neither man's schedule had permitted for an impromptu lunch or meeting for drinks.

"We've both been busy." Gideon shuffled through a stack of papers on his desk without looking up at his assistant. "I'll give him a call."

"Preferably today."

Gideon narrowed his gaze at his assistant. "How about as soon as you leave my office?"

"You've got it." Landon saluted as he rose to his feet. "Keep me posted."

As soon as Landon was gone, Gideon pulled out his cell phone and dialed his friend.

"Gideon, what's up?" Matt answered, out of breath.

"I didn't catch you in the middle of—"

"No." Matt laughed. "I took a break to work out. I was on the treadmill."

"If this is a bad time—"

"It isn't. I could use the break."

"It's about that deal in Dubai I mentioned to you before. You've been griping about missing out on my last three projects."

"True. They had killer returns. I'm still kicking

myself for not getting in on that deal in New York. The price per square foot in that neighborhood is through the roof."

"Precisely," Gideon said. "That's why I'm trying to save you a spot on this Dubai deal. The ROI is going to be even bigger than on the New York project."

"I hear exciting things about the opportunities in Dubai. But I'm a little nervous about investing in real estate internationally outside of my part-time residences. Investing in the Middle East makes me particularly apprehensive."

"Have you ever been to Abu Dhabi or Dubai?" Gideon prodded.

"Can't say I have."

"Both cities are remarkable. In fact, if you and Nadia are still debating a honeymoon destination, Dubai would be a terrific spot. It's a luxurious oasis."

Matt had recently gotten married to his former assistant, Nadia Gonzalez, but with the anniversary retreat, they'd postponed their honeymoon.

"I was thinking somewhere tropical, like Tahiti." Matt chuckled. "But I get your point. Look, I don't want to be on the outside looking in on your next big deal, but I need to know a little more about what I'd be getting myself into on this one before I'm willing to invest the kind of money you're talking about here."

"Understandable." Gideon drummed his fingers on his desk. "We're working on a fairly tight window here. So why don't we discuss the details over lunch?"

"I'm in the midst of preparing for the retreat I've

rescheduled. So I'm pretty tied up," Matt hedged. "You'll be there, right?"

"I look forward to spending time in Napa Valley."

"Come in on Thursday instead of Friday. You and I can sit down over drinks and hash this out then."

Gideon's jaw tensed. The retreat was two weeks away, making the timeline even tighter. But if he squeezed Matt on a deal he was already squirrelly on, it'd scare his friend off.

"Sounds perfect," Gideon said.

"See you in Napa Valley two weeks from now."

Gideon hung up with his friend and sighed.

Nothing worthwhile ever came easy. His entire life had been a testament to that.

Gideon scrolled through his emails and came across the invite to the retreat again. A gorgeous photo of Jessie was plastered across the graphic. He was still a sucker for those big brown eyes and that generous smile. The one that still instantly made him smile, too.

He'd begged off the Seattle retreat at the last minute, deciding it would be better if he and Jessie didn't cross paths. In the end, it didn't matter since it was canceled, but the truth was he feared Jessie hadn't forgiven him. That she wouldn't welcome a reunion. But avoiding the rescheduled retreat in Napa Valley wasn't an option. So it was better that he went in with a plan.

He needed to approach Jessie first. Wipe the slate clean and let bygones be bygones. He only hoped Jessie was inclined to do the same.

Nine

Gideon Johns walked into the lobby of The Goblet Hotel on Thursday a little after one in the afternoon. He'd arrived even earlier than Matt suggested to ensure he got a chance to sit down and chat with his friend well ahead of the start of the festivities.

"Gideon." Teresa grinned as she approached him, a wide smile spread across her face. Her gorgeous blue eyes sparkled as she shook his hand in both of hers. "It's wonderful to see you again. Matt said you would be arriving today."

Gideon leaned in closer and lowered his voice. "I realize I'm here ahead of check-in, but I'm hoping my private cottage is ready."

"I anticipated that you'd arrive prior to check-in." Teresa grinned. "Your room was ready at 10:00 a.m."

"You're amazing." Gideon smiled.

Teresa walked to the front desk with him. "Melva, this is Mr. Gideon Johns. He's the guest I requested early check-in for. He's in one of the private cottages."

Gideon handed the clerk his credit card and identification. He turned toward Teresa, lowering his voice again.

"I'm glad you're in such a good mood." Gideon didn't want to wreck her upbeat disposition by going into the specifics of the ugly rumors circulating around Seattle about her and Liam. But he wanted to assure her he didn't believe them. "You're good people, Teresa."

Her smile deepened and her eyes were filled with gratitude. She placed a hand on the forearm he'd propped on the front desk. "Thank you. That means a lot."

He'd spent most of his adult life honing his ability to read people and decipher their intentions. Nothing about Teresa St. Claire made him believe she was the scheming vixen that the haters and gossipers in his circle would have him believe her to be. But in a business like hers, perception was everything.

It was a dilemma to which he could relate.

Gideon didn't believe for an instant that Teresa had nefarious motives when it came to Liam Christopher and his family's corporation. But as he spotted Liam sitting in a chair across the lobby watching them intently, it was clear that Liam's interest in Teresa wasn't just business.

The hunger in his eyes as his gaze slid over Teresa's body spoke more of the bedroom than the boardroom. The way the man's eyes narrowed and his nostrils flared when Gideon leaned in to speak to Teresa in a hushed tone indicated the slightest hint of possession.

Regardless of what might have gone on between them, Gideon refused to believe the woman he'd gotten to know was capable of the deceit and betrayal of which she'd been accused. But in his experience, many people born of wealth liked to believe that people who came from very humble beginnings, like him and Teresa, didn't belong, regardless of how hard they'd worked or how high they'd risen. They were a social experiment waiting to implode. And when they did, they'd shake their heads and wag their tongues as they mused about their moral defectiveness.

It was the reason he felt a kinship of sorts with Teresa.

"Your business partner over there is giving me the death stare." Gideon indicated Liam's general direction with a shift of his gaze.

Teresa's cheeks flamed and she cleared her throat. "I can't imagine why."

"Can't you?" Gideon gave her a good-natured smile as he returned his credit card and ID to his wallet while the desk clerk prepared his room key. "Relax, Teresa. I don't believe any of the bullshit I've heard. But it's obvious you two care for each other. I know it doesn't seem like it right now, but my gut tells me that everything will work out for the two of you."

"Who knew the great Gideon Johns was a hopeless romantic?"

"Maybe once upon a time, but that time has long…" Gideon turned toward a beautiful brown-skinned woman wearing expensive sunglasses, a chocolate-brown silk dress and a pair of rose gold high-heel sandals with a sexy crystal bow detail. The height of the heels and the thin, barely-there straps across the ankle and toe made the one leg exposed by her dress seem a mile long.

"Jessie Humphrey?" He whispered the name beneath his breath, but Teresa, who'd followed his gaze, clearly heard him.

"I hear you two don't require an introduction." Teresa beamed, clearly amused by how distracted he was by Jessie's arrival. She nodded toward the goddess with miles of creamy skin who approached the desk.

"Jessie, I'm glad you made it. I trust that your trip was less eventful this time around." Teresa stepped past Gideon and clasped Jessie's hands, as if the two of them were old friends.

"Yes, thank you, Teresa. And thank you for arranging everything. My flight was lovely."

"Well, I'm sure you're tired after your cross-country trip. I'll get your registration started so you can check into your room right away." Teresa stepped over to the desk.

"Hello, Gideon." Jessie finally acknowledged his presence, but she didn't remove her shades. "It's been a long time, hasn't it?"

"Fifteen years." He practically whispered the words as they exchanged an awkward hug.

He'd seen her PR photos on her cover and online. He'd even watched some of her performances on video. But nothing could prepare him for how stunning this woman was in person. Her creamy brown skin was flawless and her dark brown hair was pulled back into a sleek bun.

Jessie's high cheekbones and petite nose were reminiscent of her older sister's. Yet the similarities between the two ended there.

Gideon had always thought of Jessie as Geneva's little sister, which was why he'd reacted so poorly to Jessie's unexpected kiss that rainy afternoon nearly two years after Geneva had ended their relationship. He'd hurt her feelings, and they hadn't spoken since.

But that was then.

Gideon wouldn't dare reject a kiss from the woman standing before him now.

"How've you been?" He shoved a hand in his pocket.

"Well, thank you. And you've obviously done quite well for yourself." She gave him a cursory smile before handing her credentials over to another desk clerk.

"Sir...sir..." Melva gave him a knowing smile as she handed Gideon his room keys. The woman probably thought he was a shameless groupie way past his prime.

He nodded his thanks, then turned back to Jessie. "Your voice is amazing, Jess. But you know I've always thought so."

"Thank you, Gideon," she said quietly.

"How's your family?" He wasn't asking about Geneva because he was interested in her. He asked because inquiring about the health of her family without malice was the polite thing to do. Regardless of Geneva's heartbreaking rejection or her father's cruel remarks that he would never be worthy of his daughter.

"They're fine." Her shoulders tensed and she turned toward the desk clerk. "I hope yours are, too."

Even after Jessie had stepped out of Gideon's embrace, the heat from his body wrapped itself around her like a soft, warm blanket. His subtle, deliciously masculine scent tickled her nose.

However, when Gideon asked about her family, code for her sister Geneva, the warm, fuzzy feelings ceased instantly. Leaving her with the cold, dark memories of their last interaction and how broken it had left her.

Geneva had rejected him, but she was still apparently the only Humphrey sister he was really interested in. His inquiries about her were superficial niceties.

Maybe it made her petty to give him such a cryptic response. But if he wanted to hear all about his ex, he'd have to ask her directly.

"Last I heard, Geneva was living in Europe. Switzerland, maybe?"

Jessie drew in a tight breath, but fought to keep her expression neutral. She accepted her room key from the desk clerk.

"She was for a while, but she's lived in Amsterdam for the past seven or eight years with her husband, Edmond. She's Geneva Torian now." She gave him a manufactured smile designed to protect her suddenly fragile pride. "It was nice seeing you, Gideon."

Jessie turned on her four-and-a-half-inch-tall Aminah Abdul Jillil open-toe sandals and strutted toward the elevator. The bellman, who'd stacked all of her bags onto a luggage cart, moved with her.

"Jessie, wait." Gideon caught her elbow with a gentle grip. "We haven't seen each other in more than a decade. I have an important meeting today, but I'd really like to catch up."

You mean you want to hear more about Geneva.

Jessie bit back the caustic remark that burned her tongue and gnawed at her gut. Why give Gideon the satisfaction of knowing how much his rejection hurt?

She'd be cordial, but aloof.

"I hope to line up a couple of meetings of my own." Jessie tipped her chin so her gaze met his as she slipped her arm from his loose grip. "I'm performing tomorrow and I'm still tweaking some of the material. Maybe we can catch up after my final set on Saturday night."

"Of course." His voice reminded her of the pain she'd heard in it the day her sister ended things between them. "But if you're able to free up some time to grab lunch or perhaps drinks… I'd really like that."

Jessie nodded her acknowledgment, then resumed her trek toward the elevator with the bellman in tow.

They stepped onto the elevator and Gideon stood frozen, staring at her, as the elevator doors closed. As if he'd seen a ghost.

Jessie hated that she was still hurt and angry after all this time. She shouldn't be. If anything, she should be grateful to Gideon. She owed her career to him.

The heartbreak and subsequent longing she experienced drove her to pick up a pen and write poems and eventually songs. After writing songs for small local acts, Jessie had slowly climbed the songwriting ranks and written songs for chart-topping musicians.

She'd fought for the chance to sit center stage at her piano and sing her own songs. After a successful EP, she'd accepted a contract from a big studio, but she would only agree to a single album contract because the studio hadn't been willing to give her full creative control. She'd gambled on demonstrating that she was worthy of that level of oversight before she signed another contract. Hopefully for a multi-album deal. But Jessie hadn't anticipated the cost of that freedom. Nor had she been willing to sacrifice her soul for it.

Her experience with label exec Arnold Diesman taught her not to trust a wealthy, powerful man to do her bidding or have her back. In the end, that man's only real interest was his own selfish desires.

Jessie sucked in a deep breath as the elevator opened on the second floor. She followed the bellman to her luxury balcony suite. A bold silver wallpaper with a black geometric pattern welcomed her to the elegant art deco style space. She tipped the bellman once he'd unloaded her luggage, then locked the door behind him.

Jessie slipped off the flowing brown silk Cushnie designer dress with an asymmetrical hemline that skimmed her ankles in the back but rose thigh-high over her left leg. She kicked off her shoes and slipped into a pair of comfy gray sweat shorts and a white V-neck tee. Then she sank onto the sofa in the suite's well-appointed sitting area.

Seeing Gideon after all this time had been harder than she'd imagined. Which meant that the next few days would be difficult. It would be especially hard performing in front of the man who'd first inspired her to write songs of love and loss.

Chase Stratton and Dixon Benedict had both RSVP'd for the retreat. This was her best opportunity to get Chase and Dix on board with her project. So she wouldn't allow anything to throw her off course. Least of all handsome, uber-wealthy, aging-like-fine-wine Gideon Johns.

This project had the potential to change everything for her. So she wouldn't let a teenage crush distract her from her dream.

Later that evening, after making a few last-minute adjustments to her song, Jessie pulled out her cell phone in its pink rhinestone-studded case and tapped out a quick message.

You'll never guess who just asked about you. Gideon Johns.

Gideon watched as the elevator doors closed, his pride hurt by Jessie's chilly reception. He realized she wasn't happy about the way they'd left things. But he'd done the right thing. Was Jessie really still angry with him after all these years?

He'd be the first to admit that he'd handled the situation poorly. But what he rarely admitted was why he'd gotten so angry that day. Buried beneath all the practical reasons he'd rejected Jessie's proposition was the fact that he'd been startled by the way she'd made him feel. It was something he hadn't wanted to admit, even to himself.

He'd been attracted to her. Wanted her. Feelings he'd immediately rejected. She was his ex's sister.

The last thing in the world he'd wanted was to fall for another Humphrey sister. It was still the last thing he wanted. And yet, seeing her just now, he realized that he was as susceptible to it today as he'd been back then.

Gideon ordered a glass of wine at the bar.

Jessie had always been such a sweet and gentle soul. She was a ray of sunshine that he'd missed having in his life. But the woman he'd just encountered was unlike the girl he'd once known.

Was she still angry about how he'd rejected her back then? Or had fame and ambition changed Jessie?

Back when he'd known the Humphrey sisters, Jessie and Geneva had been like night and day. Geneva was confident, assured, ambitious and a bit entitled. Jessie was sweet, shy and thoughtful. Geneva always thought of herself first, while Jessie's primary concern was the people she cared about.

It had been Jessie's most endearing quality.

But maybe Jessie was more like her older sister than he remembered.

If Jessie preferred not to revisit their past, all the better.

Besides, rekindling a friendship with Jessie would sidetrack him from his primary goal this weekend. To seal the Dubai deal with Matt Richmond. Then he'd return to Seattle and forget about his encounter with the surprisingly aloof Jessie Humphrey.

Ten

Liam walked into the bar and sat down, leaving a space between him and Gideon Johns.

"Gideon." He nodded toward the man, who could barely hold back a smirk.

"Liam." Gideon took another sip of his wine. "If you've come to give me a back-off-my-woman speech, I can save us both time. My interest in Teresa is strictly professional."

"As is mine." *Now.* That critical detail he kept to himself.

Gideon's laugh made it clear that he wasn't buying it anyway. Not even for a moment.

"Do you make a habit of staring down the men who have close conversations with your business associates?" When Liam didn't answer, Gideon set his glass down. "Didn't think so."

"I thought you were too discriminating a man to believe the gossip mill, Gideon," Liam said after he'd ordered a Manhattan.

"If you mean the rumors disparaging Teresa... I don't believe a word of them." Gideon's expression grew serious. "But the part about your relationship with her being more than just business...you're the one who told me that."

"What do you mean?" Liam turned toward Gideon.

"You sat in that chair watching the woman's every move. Scowling at any man who dared smile at her." Gideon nodded toward Teresa as she walked past the bar with a male member of the hotel staff. "You can't keep your eyes off her even now. So, a word of advice, if that's the story you're going with, you might want to take it down a notch...or ten."

Liam groaned and raked his fingers through his hair. The man was right. Though it hadn't been intentional, he hadn't been able to keep his eyes off Teresa as she flitted about the hotel. Today she wore a fitted black pantsuit that perfectly complemented her figure. The sheer black blouse beneath it had a deep neckline that had his imagination and memory working overtime. Was it any wonder his eyes had a mind of their own?

"I'm sorry if I seemed—"

"Territorial?" Gideon offered, finishing his glass of wine.

"Something like that," Liam conceded. "It's a complicated situation."

"I'm no stranger to complicated situations." Gideon ordered another glass of wine. "So no judgment here. But if you're really going with the story that it's only business between you two, you might want to rethink your approach."

"Thank you for your honesty." Liam patted the man on the shoulder, then excused himself to go to his guest cottage and return an important call.

Pangs of guilt twisted Liam's gut as he picked up the telephone to return the call to Jeremy Dutton, the man he'd assigned to comb Teresa's background. The man was much more than just a private investigator. In fact, that barely scratched the surface of just what Jeremy Dutton was capable of.

While it was true that he'd come to the conclusion that it didn't make sense for Teresa to have gone to the press, there was still a lot he didn't know about the woman. Had she been honest about the nature of her relationship with his father? Was there a hidden agenda behind her interest in him? Did she have designs on acquiring a controlling interest in Christopher Corporation? Was Dutton able to dig up anything about her father, Nigel St. Claire, working for Christopher Corporation twenty years ago?

When it came to Teresa, there were too many questions and not enough answers. Answers that he needed since, thanks to the terms of his father's will, Teresa now owned 25 percent of the stock in his family's company. They were already dealing with all of the rumors and innuendo about her relationship with his father and now him. Liam needed to ensure that there were no additional skeletons that would come crashing out of this woman's closet to plunge his family and company name into further disrepute.

Anyone in his position would do the same, for the sake of their business. But he had an additional incentive to look into Teresa. He'd been given no choice about bringing her into the company. But the fact that he kept bringing her into his bed…well, that was all on him.

He genuinely liked Teresa St. Claire, but he had millions of reasons to distrust her. Most of which were sitting in local and international banks. Still, he was inexplicably drawn to her in a way he hadn't experienced with anyone else.

Common sense dictated that he leave Teresa alone. Deal with her only as he must. But the time he'd spent with Teresa at The Goblet made him remember just how much he liked her. And she seemed just as enamored with him.

Which made him feel particularly shitty about having her investigated. Despite the fact that any sensible businessman in his position would've done the same. Still, there was a question that kept running through his brain.

What if he chose to pursue a relationship with Teresa? How would she react once she learned of the investigation? Could she ever forgive him?

Despite his initial objections, in the few short

weeks since Teresa had been a part of Christopher Corporation, she'd demonstrated that she could be an asset to the organization. But he couldn't sustain any further liabilities where Teresa was concerned.

Liam dialed the private investigator. The man answered right away.

"What've you learned?" Liam asked after exchanging a cursory greeting.

"Straight to the point." The man chuckled. "My type of client."

Liam waited without reply for the man to give him the highlights of his report on Teresa.

It essentially amounted to nada. Zip. Zilch.

What the hell was he paying this guy for? He wasn't sure if he should be extremely pleased or incredibly suspicious about the lack of dirt his investigator was able to dig up after weeks of searching. Dutton was a thorough investigator on whom he frequently relied to vet potential businesses and potential business associates.

The only thing the man could confirm was that Teresa had spent a considerable amount of time with his father.

"Keep digging," Liam said. "Everyone has secrets. If there's something there, I need to know what it is."

"It's your dime, Christopher." Dutton chuckled. "I'll keep knocking on doors and kicking over rocks for as long as you're paying me to do it."

"Fine, but be subtle about it. Discretion is everything on this one."

Liam ended the call and slipped the phone into

his pocket. He was protecting his family's interest and his heart. Still, he couldn't help feeling like he was betraying Teresa by doing so behind her back.

Liam loosened his tie and opened the doors to the patio that overlooked the vineyard. He sat at the little café table, his thoughts immediately returning to the three-hour lunch he and Teresa had enjoyed together on the property just two weeks before. A memory to which his mind often drifted.

Liam could recall nearly everything about the hours they'd spent together. What she was wearing. How she'd worn her hair. Her delectable scent. The sound of her laugh. How much he'd wanted to kiss her. How his body had craved hers as he lay in bed alone that night.

Liam sighed. He was sure Teresa was hiding something. But then, he'd been holding something back, too. A secret he hadn't dared share with anyone.

He had reason to suspect he'd been adopted.

Eleven

Jessie checked her watch after she'd steamed the dress she chose for her performance the next night. It was nearly 10:00 p.m., almost 1:00 a.m. back in New York. She was already feeling the jet lag. If she went to bed now, she could get a decent night's sleep and still work out before breakfast. Her phone rang.

Geneva.

"Hey, big sis." Jessie yawned. A signal that their call wouldn't be long. "What are you doing up this early?"

It wasn't quite 7:00 a.m. in Amsterdam.

"Where did you run into Gideon? Did he recognize you right away?" Her sister completely ignored her question.

"I'm at The Goblet. It's a—"

"Luxury hotel in Napa Valley." Her sister sounded impressed.

"You know it?"

"Who doesn't?" Geneva scoffed. "What are you doing there?"

"That gig I got to perform for billionaire Matt Richmond and a bunch of his business associates—"

"The one that got canceled because of a mudslide?" her sister said incredulously. "What about it?"

"They rescheduled the event and moved it to Napa. I'll be performing the next two nights."

"So Gideon is a friend of Matt Richmond of Richmond Industries?"

"It seems so," Jessie said through an exaggerated yawn. As if it were the least interesting piece of information she'd ever heard. "They both live in Seattle. You know the rich guys there run in the same circle."

"So what did he look like? Did he recognize you right away? After all, he hasn't seen you since I broke up with him."

Not true. But it wasn't a secret she wanted to share with her sister.

"He did recognize me right away. And he looks pretty much the same. Only more mature." *And infinitely more handsome.* A fact she didn't need to mention.

"Do you think he's as rich as the business magazines say he is?"

How the hell was she supposed to know? "I'm not a forensic accountant, Gen."

"I know, smart-ass. Tell me what he was wearing, and don't spare any of the details."

"It's not like I was cataloging his entire outfit."

A slim-cut charcoal-gray Tom Ford suit with subtle pinstripes, a crisp white shirt with a burgundy Tom Ford tie, and a pair of black leather Dolce & Gabbana shoes buffed to a high shine.

Not that she was paying attention.

"Well, what did he ask you about me? You do remember that, don't you?" Geneva said, impatiently.

"I do." How could she forget? For the first time it seemed Gideon saw her as an attractive woman. But then he'd burst any delusions she had about his interest in her by inquiring about her sister. The woman who broke his heart. "He asked how you were doing."

"And?"

Jessie sighed. "And if you were still living overseas."

That was the part that had irked her most. It meant Gideon had been keeping tabs on Geneva. Pining away for her, though her sister clearly hadn't wanted him.

"Why do you care so much, anyway? You're an old married woman, living the life abroad, remember?" Jessie teased.

Geneva suddenly got quiet. "There's something I haven't told you, Jess. Edmond and I…well, we're separated."

Jessie had moved into the bathroom and started unpacking her toiletries, but her sister's admission stopped her in her tracks. "Since when?"

Geneva was slow to respond. "The past three months."

"And you're just telling me?" She and Geneva weren't the kind of sisters who told each other everything. Still, Jess couldn't believe her sister would hold back something like that.

"We've spoken at least a dozen times over the past few months." Jessie returned to the main room of her suite and looked out the window at the surrounding vineyard, lit by strings of lights. Had she been that wrapped up in her own life that she hadn't noticed how unhappy her sister had been?

"Why didn't you say something?"

"I hoped it was only temporary. That I'd never need to worry you or Mom and Dad with this."

Jessie doubted Geneva's reasons for holding back the truth were as altruistic as she made them out to be. Like their mother, Gen had always cared about maintaining appearances.

"But you no longer believe you two will reconcile?" Jessie sank onto one of the comfy chairs in the room. "Or has the news that your old flame, billionaire Gideon Johns, inquired about you prompted that decision?"

"Don't be like that, sis," Geneva pleaded. "I know you think I'm the tough one, but this whole thing with Edmond has done a number on my ego."

"I'm sorry. I didn't mean to be…" Jessie raked her short, trim nails through her hair. "What happened? The last time I visited, you and Edmond seemed very happy."

"I thought we were happy, too. But that didn't stop Edmond from finding a younger, prettier model that made him happier."

"He cheated on you?" *It figured.*

"Don't gloat, Jess. Please. I couldn't take that right now."

"Well, for what it's worth, I'm sorry to hear it." Jessie returned to the bathroom. She needed to strip off her makeup and get ready for bed. "Will you be returning to the States?"

"I haven't given it much thought. I love my life here in Amsterdam, but I hadn't realized how inextricably it's tied to Edmond. Now that the people in our circle are being forced to take sides, it's clear that they're his friends, not mine."

"You should stay with me for a little while, as soon as I get back to New York. Or Mom and Dad would love to see you."

"Thanks. I'll think about it," Geneva said. "I have to get ready for work, and it sounds like you need to hit the sack. Love you."

"Love you, too." Jessie put her phone on the charger and got ready for bed.

Gideon's inquiry about her sister had prompted Jessie's envy, but it seemed to be just the thing her sister needed. She should be grateful to Gideon for that.

It was just as well because Gideon was only interested in Geneva.

Perhaps that was exactly how it should be.

Twelve

Gideon rose early and dressed in his workout gear, determined to get in a session before his meeting with Matt Richmond later that morning. They'd had to cancel their planned meeting over drinks the night before due to an emergency conference call Matt had to take.

Gideon walked over to the main building from his luxury cottage on the property and used his key card to access the workout facility. When he stepped inside, he was greeted by an angelic voice.

Jessie was running on a treadmill wearing a headset. Oblivious to his arrival, she was singing her heart out. Gideon couldn't help smiling. He'd always loved the unique, husky tone of her voice.

He was frozen where he stood as he surveyed her.

Jessie looked incredible in her tiny workout shorts and racerback tank.

Long, lean brown legs that seemed to go on for miles. A curvy derriere and generous breasts that bounced slightly with each movement. Her dark brown hair was piled atop her head in a high ponytail.

After Jessie's icy reception the previous afternoon, he'd planned to avoid any further interaction with her. But seeing her now, he just couldn't walk away. Jessie had once meant so much to him. He thought he'd been important to her, too. He needed to understand what had changed.

He stepped onto the treadmill beside Jessie's. She was startled, but grabbed the sides of the treadmill and recovered mid-stride.

"I'm so sorry, I didn't… Gideon. Good morning." Once she recognized him, her demeanor shifted from open and friendly to polite but shuttered. She yanked the key from her machine and it ground to a halt. "I'll leave you to your workout."

Jessie turned to leave, but he caught her elbow as he'd done the day before.

"I know you have to prepare for tonight, but if you could just give me a few minutes."

"Why?" She looked at him defiantly.

"Because I need to know why it is that I couldn't have been more thrilled to see you yesterday, but you obviously don't feel the same."

Jessie tugged her arm free, but her demeanor

softened, and he saw a glimpse of the sweet young woman he'd once adored.

A chill swept up his spine as her gaze met his.

Jessie was sexy and gorgeous. She had an incredible voice and a regal presence.

Any man would be attracted to her.

But what worried him most as he stared into those big, beautiful brown eyes was that the feelings he'd tried so hard to ignore came rushing back. Feelings he needed to shut down, for both of their sakes.

Jessie's gaze swept down Gideon's physique. He was obviously no stranger to workouts. The fitted sleeveless shirt highlighted his strong arms and broad, muscular chest. His athletic shorts showcased a firm ass, strong calves, muscular thighs and the outline of his...

She raised her eyes to his quickly, meeting his dark, penetrating gaze. The image of a young Gideon Johns was permanently burned into her brain. But fifteen years later he was more handsome than ever.

As she surveyed his fit body and handsome facial features what she felt was desire, pure and simple.

But then, her feelings for Gideon had never been as simple as her physical attraction to him.

"The last time we saw each other—" Jessie tipped her chin and folded her arms "—you made it exceedingly clear you wanted nothing to do with me."

She'd gone to Gideon's apartment. Kissed him. Admitted that she wanted him. And he'd flatly rejected her.

"I know I could've handled the situation better, but you surprised me and I overreacted. You were my ex's sister. I didn't want to cause friction between you two. And if I'm being honest, I wasn't willing to take the risk of getting involved with another Humphrey sister. Your father didn't believe I was good enough for one of his daughters. I wasn't interested in going through that again."

Jessie's central memory of that day was how harsh Gideon had been toward her. He'd yelled at her. Something he'd never done before. His eyes had been filled with what she'd perceived as anger. Now she wondered if it'd been fear. "You should've told me how you felt."

Gideon sat on a nearby weight bench. "I knew you well enough to know you would've tried to convince me otherwise. I didn't want to hurt you, Jess. But I didn't want to be hurt again either. It seemed best if we both walked away and didn't look back. I hope you can understand where my head was that day. I realize, in retrospect, that I was an ass about it. I'm sorry for that."

The sincerity in his voice and dark eyes made her chest ache.

"The resentment I've harbored since then wasn't fair to you. So I'm sorry, too, Gideon."

"I'm glad we finally had this conversation." His broad mouth quirked in a half smile. "It's something I've wanted to say to you for a long time."

"Thank you, Gideon. It really was good to see you again." Jessie turned to leave.

"Wait." He sprang to his feet, standing between her and the door. "You're still leaving? Why?"

"I was practically done with my workout anyway." She folded her arms, her gaze not meeting his.

Gideon had glanced at her machine. He folded his arms, too. "You had thirty minutes left."

She smoothed back her hair. "I'm on a tight schedule this morning. I have to grab breakfast and get some practice time in on the piano I'm performing on tonight. Then I hope to wrangle a meeting with a couple of music execs who'll be here this weekend."

"Chase Stratton and Dixon Benedict?"

"Yes. How'd you—"

"I overheard Teresa talking to her assistant about them. Neither of them has arrived. Stratton's studio session got extended another day and Benedict is coming in a day late."

"Oh." Jessie's heart sank. She didn't regret taking the gig. The payday was more than generous and she was grateful for the chance to have this conversation with Gideon.

But this retreat was her best chance of connecting with her two dream producers.

"Look, if meeting them means that much to you, I'll talk to Matt. I'm sure he can arrange some—"

"No." The word came out more harshly than she'd intended. After all, Gideon only wanted to help.

He frowned, confused by her objection.

"I mean…thank you, but no. I prefer to do this on my own."

"I admire your spirit and determination, Jessie. But if I can do this for you—"

"Then I'd owe you."

Jessie hadn't meant to say the words aloud, especially not so bitterly. Her face stung with heat, remembering the day Arnold Diesman had offered to give her complete creative control on her next album, if only she'd play the game.

She'd considered Arnold a friend and mentor until the moment he'd tried to convince her that quid pro quos were the way things were done in the industry. That it wasn't a big deal.

"When I reach the pinnacle in my career, it'll be because I earned it. Not because I knew the right exec or because I'm beholden to a billionaire."

Gideon's thick, neat brows came together. He stepped aside. "I'm sorry I offended you."

Guilt knotted Jessie's gut. Gideon was a good guy who wanted to do a wonderful thing for her. She appreciated that. But doing this on her own was important to her, and she needed to spell that out to Gideon in no uncertain terms.

"You didn't offend me. I just need you to understand my position on this." After a few moments of awkward silence between them, she jerked a thumb over her shoulder toward the door. "I'd better go."

"Wait, Jess." He stalked over to where she stood near the door. "If you want to do this on your own, I respect that. Hell, I even admire it. But that doesn't mean two old friends can't catch up over breakfast, does it?"

Jessie turned to Gideon.

God, he's handsome.

He seemed eager to absolve himself of any guilt where she was concerned.

"I could meet you at the restaurant in an hour."

He glanced at his watch and frowned. "I have a business meeting then. What about now?"

"I'm not going to the restaurant looking a hot, sweaty mess. I have my public persona to consider." She smoothed her hair back.

Gideon nodded thoughtfully and shoved his hands in his pockets. The move pulled the panel of fabric tight over his crotch and inadvertently drew her eye there. "Room service in my room?"

Oh. My. Gawd.

Her entire body flushed with heat and she resisted the urge to fan herself with her open hand. When Jessie raised her gaze to his, he'd caught her checking him out.

He was more than a little pleased with himself. The smirk on his face reminded her too much of the one on Arnold's face the day he'd invited her up to his suite to strategize the direction of her career.

It was like an icy shower had been turned on over her head.

She wouldn't make the same mistake again.

"I don't think that's a good idea. How about breakfast in the restaurant tomorrow at eight?"

"Sounds good." He pulled out his phone and added their breakfast date to his calendar. He assessed her tentatively. "We should exchange numbers.

In case there's a last-minute change of plans for either of us."

Jessie rattled off her cell phone number.

He sent her a text message. "That's me. Call me if there's a change in your plans or…anything." A broad, genuine smile spanned his handsome face.

Jessie's heart danced. She was as drawn to him now as she'd been then.

Thirteen

Gideon folded the burgundy pocket square and placed it in the front pocket of his suit. Tonight's festivities would officially be under way in just a few minutes. He removed a pair of platinum cuff links from their felt jewelry box and pushed one through the hole of his custom-tailored dress shirt. He'd just put the other cuff link in place when his cell phone rang.

He checked the screen.

Landon.

Gideon answered the phone and put it on speaker before returning it to the bathroom counter. "What's up, Land?"

"Mr. Johns…"

Oh shit. This wasn't going to be good.

"I'm sorry to bother you while you're at the re-treat," he continued. "But I'm afraid I have a bit of bad news."

"Is another investor considering bailing on the project?"

"No. I think I've done a good job of addressing any concerns they may have had."

"Then what is it?"

"Some issues have come to light regarding the owner of the construction company whose bid we planned to go with. I know his bid was considerably less, but concerns are now being raised about the quality of his work. Complaints that weren't available when we did our preliminary groundwork. Even if it turns out that the information is false—"

"There'll still be the perception that the builder employs shoddy materials and workmanship." Gideon cursed under his breath. "We have no choice but to go with option two."

"Which is nearly ten percent higher than the ini-tial bid. We'll also need a bigger contingency."

Gideon's head was starting to pound. "Of course."

"I don't mean to push, but have you had the op-portunity to sit down with Matt Richmond?"

"There's been a lot going on." It was an excuse he'd call bullshit on if one of his employees had of-fered it. But his breakfast meeting with Matt had been interrupted when his friend's assistant alerted him to a problem at Richmond Industries' Miami office. "We still have a few days, so don't panic, Landon. Besides, we have a bigger issue."

"Even if Matt says yes, I doubt you anticipate getting the full remaining investment from him," Landon said. "And the total amount needed has just escalated." The man was silent for a few minutes. "Mr. Johns… I've been thinking. In light of everything that's been going on with this deal…maybe the timing just isn't right for it."

"It's the nature of the beast, Landon," Gideon said calmly. "It doesn't matter if it's a tiny residential rehab, a towering skyscraper or a commercial complex. Shit happens. Sometimes it's a little. Sometimes it's a lot. And the bigger the risk, the more shit is going to hit the fan. It's as simple as that."

"So you're not worried?"

"It's my job to worry. I do that whether we're behind the eight ball or way ahead of the game." Gideon checked his watch. He needed to get over to the main building for the welcome party. He didn't want to miss Jessie's performance. "Your only worry should be doing your job and doing it well. Everything else will be fine. Now, I've got this under control. Go out and enjoy your weekend. We'll hit the second-tier potential investor list hard on Monday morning."

Landon agreed, sounding more upbeat.

Gideon ended the call, straightened his tie and got ready to join the party.

Gideon stepped onto the patio of The Goblet. The tented space was elegantly decorated. The patio was overflowing with some of the most elite and powerful captains of industry in the fields of technology, information science, entertainment and more. A four-piece live band stood on the stage playing soft jazz.

"Good evening, Gideon." Teresa grinned as she approached him. "What do you think?"

The woman had traded her usual pantsuit for an elegant silver dress with a low-cut back and crystal detailing on the front. Her blond hair fell to her shoulders in soft, beachy waves. She stood beside him and admired her work. It was one of the few times in the past two days that he hadn't seen the woman moving so fast on her designer high heels that she was practically a blur.

"It's quite lovely, Teresa. I'm impressed, especially since you've done this on such short notice." Gideon accepted a glass of red wine from a passing server and took a sip. "And holding the event at a boutique hotel with a working vineyard. That was a stroke of genius."

"It was, but sadly, I can't take credit for the selection of the location. It was Liam Christopher who suggested it." She nodded toward Liam, who stood on the far side of the patio, eyeing them.

The man acknowledged them with a quick nod. Then he averted his gaze and moved to talk to another partygoer. A beautiful redhead wearing a long, flowing green gown.

The slightest frown furrowed Teresa's brow.

Neither of them is exactly subtle. No wonder rumors are flying about them.

"I'd like to keep this venue on the map for a real estate investor retreat I'm planning next year. I'm focused on another project right now, but give me a call in a few weeks. I'd like to do some preliminary planning. You did such an amazing job at my last party. You are the only event planner I ever want to use."

Teresa beamed. She tapped out a memo on her cell phone. "I'll have Corinne give Landon a call later next week."

She nodded toward her assistant, who spoke animatedly to a member of the hotel staff. The woman wore a long, simple black gown. Her corkscrew red curls were pulled into a low bun.

The mention of his assistant reminded him this wasn't just a social call. He needed to nail down Matt Richmond's investment and identify a handful of smaller investors.

Teresa excused herself to go and speak with one of her staff members.

Gideon finished his drink, then moved toward Matt and Nadia, who stood together near the center of the party. Now wasn't the time to pin Matt down. But he could continue to sow seeds of interest and perhaps reel in other potential investors.

He was embroiled in a lively conversation with Matt, Nadia and two other guests when Jessie Humphrey swept into the space. She was stunning, stealing his breath away in the midst of a conversation about his most recent visit to Dubai and the building explosion there.

The flowing red floor-length gown had a simple but lovely top with a deep vee that showed off the buttery smooth skin of her toned brown shoulders.

The bottom portion of the dress boasted intricate beading over a sheer fabric that overlaid the satin skirt beneath it. The dress commanded attention and partygoers gave her a wide berth as she moved about. He'd venture that their reaction was as much because of the incredible beauty of this woman in her stunning ball gown as because of her celebrity status.

"Someone is certainly an admirer." Matt chuckled. "Pretty sure I've never seen you speechless before." He leaned in closer so only Gideon and Nadia could hear him. "I could introduce you."

"Not necessary." Gideon loosened his tie and cleared his throat. Suddenly the space seemed much hotter than it had been before Jessie arrived. "We're already acquainted. In fact, we have a breakfast date tomorrow morning."

Matt's and Nadia's eyes widened.

"There must be a story there." Nadia smiled. "Why don't I take these gentlemen to meet our guest of honor. That should give you a chance to tell it."

Matt gave his wife a quick kiss on the cheek before she ushered the other men toward Jessie.

"Nadia is working with Teresa now, isn't she?" Gideon inquired.

"As a contractor, not an employee. But not at this event. Teresa insisted that she should just enjoy the event with her husband. And I couldn't agree more. But don't change the subject," his friend teased. "You certainly didn't waste any time getting to know Jessie Humphrey."

"Actually, I've known Jessie for many years," he

clarified. "I dated her older sister, Geneva, when we were teenagers."

"Well, baby sis is all grown up now." Matt nodded toward her.

Amen to that.

Gideon sighed without response, his eyes trailing Jessie as she flitted about the room meeting party-goers.

She is so damn beautiful.

A partial updo allowed soft spirals to spill down one side of her lovely face. Her makeup was perfect. Naturally luminescent rather than overly done. Her eyes sparkled and her teeth gleamed as she flashed her brilliant smile or launched into the contagious laugh he remembered so fondly.

The woman was mesmerizing and she exuded confidence, which made her sexier still.

He was in serious danger of falling for her.

Jessie smiled and nodded as she mingled with a few of the guests before her performance. It was part of her contract.

Not that she wouldn't have mingled with the party-goers anyway. She'd just prefer to wait until after she'd performed, so that she could remain focused.

Despite being most comfortable onstage in front of an intimate audience, she still tended to get nervous before she performed. But the jitters she felt and the fluttering in her belly had more to do with the tall, dark, handsome man standing on the other side of the room staring at her.

Jessie hadn't met Gideon's gaze, but she'd angled her head so that she could study him. His tasteful black suit, complete with vest, fit his large, muscular frame well. A burgundy tie and pocket square were the perfect choice. And the shoes…gradient burgundy and black oxfords with an elegant style and shape that made her reasonably sure they were a pair of Corthays.

"Will you be performing songs from your current album tonight, Jessie?" a beautiful blonde woman in an elegant white dress asked eagerly.

"A few." Jessie kept a smile plastered on her face. It was a sore point. Of course people wanted to hear her perform the bubbly pop hits that they'd heard on the radio. But that wasn't what she wanted to play. "At an intimate event like this, I try to provide something you can't experience listening to a Top 40 pop station. So I'll also be performing new material."

The woman squealed, gripping the arm of the handsome man accompanying her. "I can't wait to tell all my friends I was one of the first people to hear Jessie Humphrey perform an original song. Would you mind taking a selfie with me?"

"Not at all." Jessie smiled graciously and stood beside the woman.

This part never got old. Sure, there were times when she just wanted to sit in peace and enjoy her dinner or get onto a plane in her sweats and baseball cap without being spotted. But in those inconvenient moments she always reminded herself to remain grateful. And she remembered how badly she'd wanted her name on that marquee, instead of solely in the songwriting credits.

After taking several photos together, the woman thanked her.

"You look absolutely stunning, Jessie."

Her spine stiffened at the sound of the smooth, honeyed voice that washed over her and made her pulse race and her spine tingle.

"Good evening, Gideon." She turned to face him.

The man was even more handsome up close, and he smelled absolutely divine. Jessie had the urge to lean forward, press a hand to his broad chest and inhale his delectable scent.

He bent toward her and whispered in her ear, "You're the most beautiful woman in this room, and you are incredibly talented. You're going to kill it tonight."

Jessie's face warmed as she inhaled his masculine scent and absorbed the heat radiating from his body. She smoothed down her skirt with trembling hands.

"Thank you, Gideon." Her words were soft, meant only for him. "You saying that…it means a lot to me."

"I'm only stating the obvious." Gideon seemed pleased by her admission. "Look, I know you have to mingle with the crowd, but I'd love to buy you a drink and chat later, if you have time."

"That would be wonderful." Jessie gave him a reserved smile, then watched as he disappeared into the crowd. Her body tingled with desire for this man. That certainly hadn't changed. But getting involved with Gideon was a bad idea.

* * *

The sun had just gone down when Jessie sat on the bench in front of the gleaming baby grand piano. Matt Richmond had introduced her and escorted her onto the small stage. She scanned the glamorous, well-dressed crowd of people eagerly anticipating her performance.

She hadn't seen Chase Stratton or Dixon Benedict in attendance at the event yet. It was disappointing, but it wouldn't change how she approached her performance. She would be authentic and give the audience her very best, leaving it all on the stage.

That was her policy for every performance, be it as the opening act on a stadium stage or in a small club that could barely accommodate a baby grand piano.

Jessie started to play the chorus of an older song of hers that she didn't intend to sing. She leaned into the microphone mounted over the piano.

"How are we doing tonight, beautiful people?" she asked in a soft, intimate rasp that prompted the crowd to shout variations of *good* or *fine*.

"That didn't sound very convincing, now did it?" she teased. The crowd laughed in response. "Why don't we try this one more time. I said, how are you incredibly beautiful people feeling on this amazing starry night?"

The crowd shouted back more enthusiastically.

"Now that's what I'm talking about." She nodded. "And are we having a good time tonight?"

The audience shouted back *yes,* many of them holding their drinks up as they did.

She started the set by playing snippets of a few of the songs she'd written for top acts. Something that always got the crowd going. Then she amped up the party by playing a couple of the songs from her recent album that had made it onto the pop charts.

Jessie played the bluesy intro from her first EP as a bridge to the emotional, deeply sentimental songs she'd play next.

"This next song is one of the first songs I ever wrote." Jessie continued to play the piano as she spoke. "I was a shy teenager and I'd had my heart broken for the first time." The audience *aw*-ed in unison. "I know, right? We've all been there. But it wasn't all bad. Because if it hadn't happened, I don't know if I'd be sitting here with you tonight."

Many people in the audience nodded as if they could relate.

"So I picked up my scented gel pen." The audience laughed. "Hey, I was still a teenager, y'all." She laughed, too. "But I picked up this pen and I decided to write some poetry. I wrote my little heart out and it was…trash." She laughed. "Utter and complete garbage. I filled two wastebaskets trying to get my thoughts on paper in a way that empowered me and healed my broken heart just the tiniest bit. Eventually, I wrote something that felt right, except it didn't quite feel complete."

She dramatically played the chords that made up the chorus of the song she was going to sing, and people cheered and clapped with recognition. Then she returned to playing the intro.

"It needed that little oomph. It needed music. The kind of music that touches people's souls. So I converted my sad little love poem into lyrics, and I wrote the bars of the chorus. The rest worked itself out from there. So if you've ever had your heart broken, if you've ever needed someone to remind you that no matter how bad it feels right now, it's not the end of the world, this song is for you." She scanned the crowd, pleased by their enthusiastic responses.

"The sun will shine again tomorrow. And when you wake up, in all of your fabulousness…" She waved one hand over the crowd. "You'll get the chance to eventually get it right. Whether it be with the same person—" her gaze involuntarily met Gideon's "—or with someone new."

Jessie launched into the opening bars of "Next Time I'll Get It Right," her voice strong and clear. She sang the song with every bit of her heart and soul. Just the way she'd written it. It gutted her every time she told the story of this song. Every time she performed it. But tonight it felt surreal, performing the song that had launched her songwriting and eventually her singing career. Knowing the man who'd inspired it was standing in the crowd, just a few feet away.

Fourteen

Jessie's pulse raced after the extended applause from the audience at the end of her performance. Regardless of how many people were in the crowd or how long she'd been doing this, an enthusiastic response was always exhilarating.

Matt Richmond returned to escort her off the stage. He and Nadia were gracious hosts.

She'd taken official photos with them before she'd gone onstage. Afterward, they both raved over how much they enjoyed her performance. Nadia even confessed that back when she was hopelessly in love with Matt, who also happened to be her boss, she'd taken solace in Jessie's songs.

Jessie returned to the party to mingle and take photos with many of Matt Richmond's business friends. After taking what felt like her hundredth selfie of the night, she was finally standing alone. Gideon, who'd been watching from his perch on a barstool all evening, approached her.

"I've been listening to your albums for the past few weeks, and I have to tell you, I didn't think you could possibly top the recordings. But that live performance was brilliant. It was intimate and gut-wrenching. Yet you left us on a positive note. It was truly outstanding."

"You've listened to my music?" Jessie had never given thought to whether Gideon was out there in the world listening to her music. He'd loved rock and hip-hop. What she sang was neither.

"Absolutely. I'm not stalking you on social media or anything, but I've followed your career enough to know you've written some pretty damn amazing songs for the biggest artists out there. You're unbelievably talented, Jessie. Guess those piano lessons your parents made you take paid off after all." He chuckled softly.

"Guess they did." Jessie couldn't help smiling, remembering how she'd whined and complained because Geneva didn't have to take lessons. "Of course, they're disappointed that I'm not making *real* music." She used air quotes.

Gideon's expression soured. His voice was suddenly tight. "How are Mr. and Mrs. Humphrey?"

He grabbed two glasses of champagne from a passing server and handed her one.

"As pretentious as ever." She accepted the champagne flute with a bitter laugh. "Though my mother isn't above musing to her friends about just how close she came to having a billionaire for a son-in-law."

Gideon frowned. "I doubt your father shares that viewpoint."

Jessie sipped the bubbly liquid. It tickled her nose.

"My father believes that had he not deemed you unsuitable for his daughter, you'd never have developed the drive to become a self-made billionaire." She hated repeating her father's words, but she wouldn't lie to Gideon. Besides, after his history with Milton Humphrey, she couldn't imagine that he'd have expected anything less of him.

"I've often contemplated that very thing." Gideon took a healthy sip of his champagne. He shrugged. "Maybe he's right."

"I don't believe that for a minute. Look at what you've accomplished over the last fifteen years. I refuse to give my father credit for all of that."

"I'm not saying I would be in the same situation I was born into. I know I would've made something of my life, if for no other reason than I loved your sister and would've done anything to give her the life to which she was accustomed. But this…" He took another sip. "I suppose I should thank your father for proclaiming me unworthy of his daughter."

They stood together quietly, drinking champagne and watching the crowd move around them.

Jessie set her empty champagne flute on a passing tray and rearranged the large flowing skirt of her beautiful designer dress. The ballroom gown took up so much space between them. But perhaps that was a good thing. It gave her room to breathe in a space where his close proximity and subtle masculine scent already seemed to overwhelm her.

The band had set back up and started to play again. Couples were filing onto the dance floor.

Gideon set his empty champagne flute on a nearby tray, then extended his large palm to her. "Care to dance?"

Jessie's gaze went from his offered hand to his incredibly handsome face and the dark, penetrating eyes that seemed to look right through her.

She couldn't speak. She nodded, placing her smaller hand in his, and followed him onto the crowded dance floor.

Gideon took Jessie in his arms and they swayed to the music in silence. He still found it hard to believe that the woman he was holding in his arms now was the same sweet, awkward girl with the big smile and beautiful spirit he'd once known.

It'd been one thing to see Jessie in a video or on an album cover. But standing with her now felt surreal.

It felt odd to be swaying with the beautiful woman she'd become and feeling such a deep attraction to her. And she was obviously still attracted to him.

His relationship with Geneva had ended long ago and she'd certainly moved on. He saw no reason he and Jessie couldn't explore their feelings.

"I guess I should thank you for not outing me as the lout who broke your heart back then." His lips grazed her ear as he leaned down and whispered the words in her ear.

"You're assuming you were the impetus for the song." Her back tensed beneath his fingertips. "I never said that."

"True." He nodded. "But I've been listening to the lyrics from that EP. It reminded me of conversations we've had."

"I write songs as a way to tell my story, not as a way to humiliate anyone else." She met his gaze. "I'm not a fan of revenge songs. Mostly because the people who've become famous for them tend to have a thin skin when the tables are turned."

"I agree," he said. "But I'm grateful just the same. I'd hate to become known as the cad that broke Jessie Humphrey's heart. Especially since it's the last thing I ever intended to do."

"I realize that now." Jessie dropped her gaze.

"What happened that day prompted you to become a songwriter. Just like your father's harsh dismissal set me on my path." He smiled faintly. "I guess there's some truth to those clichés."

"Like when one door closes, another opens," Jessie volunteered. "That was my grandmother's favorite."

"Mine, too." He smiled, thinking of the woman who'd meant so much to him. "We were destined to take separate paths, but I'm grateful they've crossed again."

"So am I." Jessie's eyes glistened with emotion as they danced beneath the stars.

He held her closer and she laid her head on his chest as they moved together.

She smelled like a field of flowers in spring and it felt good to hold her body against his. The attraction he'd felt for Jessie when he'd first seen her yesterday afternoon had only grown stronger.

He was glad they'd cleared the air. Perhaps they'd laid the foundation upon which they could rebuild their friendship. But as he held her in his arms, it was impossible to deny that he wanted more than just friendship with Jessie. If they could manage it without damaging this fragile thing they were rebuilding.

There was something about this beautiful young woman with an old soul who touched people's hearts. He wanted more than just a night or two with Jessie. But he had no reason to believe she wanted the same.

Jessie was thrilled Gideon was happy about their unplanned reunion.

She certainly hadn't felt that way initially. A feeling that was compounded by his inquiry about their family, in what she'd suspected was a sly bid for information about her sister.

But nothing about their conversations since made her believe Gideon was angling for a chance to renew his relationship with Geneva. So perhaps she'd been wrong. Especially since his reaction to her yesterday and tonight made it clear he was attracted to her.

She'd concentrated so much of her energy on her anger toward Gideon. But once that raw, jagged emotion dissipated, her heart was filled with the warmth and affection she'd once had for him.

Jessie had been thinking of him since their encounter in the gym that morning.

How would Gideon react if she kissed him tonight?

She was no longer a teenage girl crushing on her older sister's ex. She was a grown woman fully capable of entering into a consensual fling.

And that's all it would be.

Gideon had his life in Seattle. She had hers back in New York. But the desire to be with him burned strong. He was still the man she compared every other man to in the back of her head.

"You told me that Geneva is married, but you didn't tell me anything about yourself. Is there a special guy waiting for you back home?"

"No." Jessie's spine tingled, hope filling her chest. "What about you? Is there a Mrs. Gideon Johns?"

Gideon laughed, as if it were a ridiculous question. "No," he said finally. "Maybe that's because I've been so focused on chasing the next deal."

"With all the success you've had, I'm surprised you're not thinking of retiring to some tropical island. Maybe starting a family. And you've never been married."

Jessie wanted to take back those last words as soon as she'd uttered them.

"So you've been checking up on me?" Gideon grinned.

"Only after we talked in the gym this morning.

And I might have a financial magazine or two at home with your face on them."

"Somehow it makes me feel better that, even when you were angry with me, some part of you still cared enough to wonder what was going on in my life. I've always wondered about yours."

"And Geneva's," she said. It wasn't a question. He'd known her sister had lived in Switzerland. His information just hadn't been up to date.

"And Geneva," he repeated the words. "There was a time ten years ago, after I'd made my first million in real estate, that I wondered if there wasn't still a chance for us. I considered calling her up."

"Did you?" Jessie stared at him intensely.

"No. I flew to Zurich instead, planning to surprise her and sweep her off her feet."

A knot tightened in Jessie's stomach. "What happened?"

"I went to see her with a big bouquet of flowers in hand. But as I approached her flat I saw her with someone else. It was obvious he'd spent the night and she was seeing him off. I felt foolish for making the trip. For assuming that she'd want me."

"So you never really got over her. Is that why you never married? Because you were holding out hope that you and Geneva would eventually get back together?"

"No." The denial wasn't nearly as convincing as his earlier one. "We were never meant to be. I've made peace with that."

Jessie's gaze snapped to his. "What if Geneva weren't married?"

"She is."

"What if she weren't?" Jessie insisted.

"What I felt for Geneva…that was a long time ago. Truthfully, your sister was right. We wanted different things in life, even then."

Jessie gnawed on her lower lip in silence as she stared at the handsome man who held her in his arms.

What if she could finally trade her fantasies and what-ifs for a night in Gideon's arms? In his bed?

It was a thought that had consumed her all afternoon. But if Gideon still had a thing for Geneva, she'd be setting herself up for heartache, despite her intention to walk away at the end of their weekend.

Besides, she'd spent one evening with Gideon and she was already allowing his presence to distract her from her focus. She was here to convince Chase and Dixon to work on her project. But she'd spent the entire night drowning in Gideon's eyes and fawning over him.

"Thank you for the dance, Gideon. I should mingle with some of the other guests." She pulled out of his embrace. "And I need to check with Teresa to see if Chase or Dixon has arrived."

"Of course." He nodded, shoving a hand in his pocket. "I won't be able to make it for breakfast tomorrow morning due to an important business meeting. Maybe we could have a nightcap later?"

Jessie wanted to accept his offer. To whisper in his ear exactly what she'd imagined so many times.

But it would be a mistake. When he learned that Geneva would soon be free, he'd choose her instead.

"It's been a long day and I'm still jet-lagged. Another time maybe?"

"Sure." Gideon smiled, but his eyes revealed his disappointment. He kissed her cheek. "Good night, Jess."

She made her way to the other side of the covered patio, away from Gideon Johns.

Fifteen

Gideon watched Matt's reaction as the man surveyed the prospectus that Landon had put together for him on the Dubai deal. After trying to meet with Matt twice already this weekend, he'd arranged for them to have room service breakfast at his private cottage.

It was the best way for Gideon to minimize the interruptions as he tried to finalize Matt's participation in the deal.

"How much do you have on the line on this one?" Matt asked calmly as he sipped his coffee.

"Everything." Even Gideon was taken aback by his frank response.

He wasn't one to rely on a pitiful song and dance in order to get investors on board. Not even when the potential investor happened to be a friend.

"Not monetarily, of course," Gideon added when Matt regarded him skeptically. "But my reputation and the future of my company are riding on this deal. I won't lie to you, Matt. A couple of major investors pulled out recently. Not because of anything having to do with the deal itself. This deal is solid. We've done our homework on this and expect to see one of our greatest returns to date."

"Then why'd those two investors pull out of the deal?" Matt folded his arms, his brows knitted.

"Both men were spooked by volatilities in their industry. Teaches me a lesson going forward. Don't rely too heavily on investors from a single business sector. If market changes negatively impact that industry, the deal could go under."

"Makes sense." Matt nodded. "But I'm looking to invest ten million max in this deal. How do you plan to make up the shortfall?"

"Landon and I have been working the phones tirelessly for the past two weeks. We've secured most of the required funding for this deal. Once you're on board, I'll just need a few additional investments."

"And?" Matt looked up from cutting into his omelet.

"I've got phone meetings lined up for those this afternoon." Gideon took a bite of his crepe. He spoke calmly.

No pressure.

Despite the fact that he needed Matt's investment in order to complete this deal, his friend wouldn't be making this commitment as some favor to him.

It was an excellent opportunity for Richmond Industries to make an awful lot of money. That's what he'd focused on during his presentation to Matt. The solid return this deal offered with a relatively quick turnaround.

Matt picked up the prospectus and thumbed through it again in silence. Gideon didn't interrupt. He just kept eating his crepe and drinking his orange juice. As if all of this were no big deal.

"Okay." Matt put the folder down and looked squarely at Gideon. "I'm in. Send the paperwork to my office. Our attorneys will review it and then we'll cut you a check. Anything else I need to do?"

"No. We'll make this as convenient for you as we can," Gideon said nonchalantly. "The paper work will be waiting for you when you return to Seattle."

Matt shook his hand. "I look forward to finally doing business with you. It's been a long time coming."

"It has." Gideon kept his voice even, despite wanting to do a victory dance worthy of an end zone. "Welcome aboard."

"Speaking of something being a long time coming, it seems that your reunion with Jessie Humphrey was worth the wait." Matt took the final bite of his omelet.

"It's been great seeing her again. We were able to clear the air. Hopefully we'll rebuild our friendship."

"Friendship?" Matt's eyebrows drew together. "I saw how you were looking at her. Seemed like more than friendship to me. A couple of guys asked if you two were an item. They were hoping to ask her out."

"Who wanted to ask her out?" A knot formed in his gut and his hands clenched into fists.

"See, that face right there—" Matt laughed as he pointed to him "—that's definitely jealousy. You want to tell me again how she's just a friend?"

Gideon cut another piece of his crepe without responding. No need to add fuel to the fire. Matt was already enjoying this way too much.

"It's more serious than I thought." Matt finished his coffee. "You usually have a much better poker face. I should know. I've lost to you enough times because of it. Does Jessie know?"

"Does she know what?" Gideon tried not to be irritated with his friend. After all, the man had probably just saved his Dubai deal. "That I want to be friends again?"

"That you see her as more than a friend or a weekend hookup. I've seen you with both. Neither has ever produced anything nearly as intense as the vibe you're giving off right now or the aura surrounding you two on the dance floor last night."

"Vibes? Auras? Really, Matt?" Gideon teased his friend. "Next you'll be telling me the stars aligned to bring us together this weekend."

"Sounds more like something Nadia would say than me, but I can't disagree. Maybe this was the whole point of that disastrous mudslide at the original event. If that's the case, I've got a pretty hefty bill I'd like to send you." Matt climbed to his feet.

"Ha, ha, ha." Gideon stood, too. "You're a regular comedian."

"Nope. I'm just a guy in love who recognizes it when I see it in another guy. Especially one who still has no clue that he's already in over his head." Matt smiled broadly. "I have to prepare for my presentation with Liam later this morning. So I'd better go. Thanks for breakfast and for bringing me in on this deal. I'm excited about it."

"One more thing." Gideon drew in a deep breath, knowing he shouldn't ask but unable to stop himself. "The two music producers who are here—"

"Dixon Benedict and Chase Stratton. What about them?" Matt frowned. "Looking for more investors?"

"No, it's nothing like that. Do you think you'd be able to arrange a meeting with the two of them?"

Matt smirked knowingly. "You mean do I think I could secure a meeting for Jessie with the two of them?"

If he wanted to prove to Matt that he wasn't into Jessie he was doing a shit job of it. "Yeah."

"I'll see what I can do." Matt shook his hand again and left.

Gideon was as disturbed by Matt's observation about him and Jessie as he was excited to tell Landon they were close to finishing the deal.

Jessie was smart and beautiful and she made him laugh. Of course he was interested in her. He'd thought a lot about what would happen if she tried to kiss him again.

This time, he wouldn't stop her.

The image of Jess lying in his bed beneath him had kept him up, tossing and turning, all night.

Gideon grabbed his phone off the coffee table and dialed Landon. He would focus on the business at hand and let things with Jessie take their natural course.

Whatever that might be.

Jessie sat at the piano playing one of the songs she'd written for her new album. She was still tweaking the key in which she should sing it.

Teresa had confirmed that both Chase Stratton and Dixon Benedict had arrived at The Goblet the previous evening. She didn't think either of them had been there for Jessie's performance. But Teresa expected both men to be at the gala that evening and had promised to get them a table in front of the stage.

Jessie needed to deliver the performance of her life and impress both men. And she needed to stay laser-focused on her primary reason for taking this gig: securing the funding and ideal producers for her independent album.

She'd chosen to bet on herself, rather than accept a soul-sucking record deal. Or trade her integrity for the deal she wanted. *Everything* was riding on this project.

She wanted to create a collection of songs that would become part of the soundtrack of people's lives. If she succeeded, labels would be knocking down the door to offer her a deal. And she would establish her right to retain creative freedom on future projects.

The album needed to be brilliant enough to receive critical nods and outsell her last album, despite limited distribution. It was a skyscraper-tall order. But big-name producers like Chase and Dixon could help her get wider distribution than she could on her own, even with her past success.

She needed to remember what was at stake tonight for her career rather than obsessing over Gideon. What he meant to her then. The mistakes they'd both made fifteen years ago. How he'd react if she proposed a weekend tryst.

Jessie sucked in a deep breath, her head spinning as her hands moved across the keys. She hit the wrong note, then banged on the piano keys in frustration.

She couldn't lose focus, lost in thoughts of Gideon. It was a cruel catch-22, because the song she hoped to wow Chase and Dixon with was one that had been inspired by Gideon's rejection that day. Born of all the pain, hurt and anger she'd felt and the realization that it was time to let it all go and move on.

It was ironic that he'd waltz back into her life after she'd written that song. The universe had one hell of a sense of humor.

"Okay" was the most raw, emotional song she'd written to date. She needed to tap into the pain and loss she'd felt that day. And she had to transport the audience to that place where they could connect to their own experiences of love and loss.

It had been unnerving to perform with Gideon in the audience last night. Especially when she'd introduced the song that had clearly been about her feelings for him. But tonight, most of her planned set featured songs that would force her to relive those intense feelings. She'd be playing them all out in front of the man who'd inspired them.

She couldn't hold back any of those raw emotions. Her authentic sound and poignant delivery were what set her apart from her pop diva peers. So she would lean into whatever feelings arose and ride the wave of those emotions.

A piece of her hoped Gideon didn't show tonight. Then she could lay her heart out on the stage for everyone except him to see.

She doubted she would be that lucky.

The only thing that mattered was that Chase and Dixon would be there for the performance. They needed to understand what she was capable of. If she could manage that, she wouldn't need to convince them. They'd be clamoring to work with her.

"Jessie, is everything all right with the piano?" Teresa approached her with a platter containing a mug of tea and a saucer. "You're certainly deep in thought."

Jessie hadn't realized she'd stopped playing. She was sitting there as if the entire world weighed on her shoulders.

No wonder Teresa was worried.

"Everything is good. Thank you." Jessie took a sip of the warm chamomile tea the woman handed her. "In terms of attention to detail and anticipating the needs of the guests, you're one of the best event planners I've worked with. If you weren't on the West

Coast, I'd hire you to plan the album release party once I'm done."

"Thank you, Jessie." Teresa beamed. "And thank you for agreeing to do this event. After the disaster at The Opulence, I wouldn't have blamed you if you'd turned me down."

"Well, you did sweeten the deal." Jessie laughed. "I can't thank you enough for getting Chase and Dixon in the room for tonight's performance."

"I'm glad we could make it happen. If you give them even half of what you gave us last night, they'll both be *begging* to work with you." Teresa looked up when the banquet manager called her name. "I'd better go. Call me if you need anything. We want to build up the drama of your performance tonight, so don't mingle with the guests beforehand this time. Let's save it until after your set. If you could arrive in the staging area about an hour before go time, we'll make sure everything is ready."

Jessie thanked Teresa. Then when she had the space to herself again, she closed her eyes and let her fingers travel over the keys.

Sixteen

Teresa stood at the back of the auditorium late Saturday morning as Matt and Liam sat at the center of the stage concluding their talk on their new joint AI venture, the Sasha Project. The room was nearly filled to capacity. At the end of their presentation, they were greeted by thunderous applause.

The retreat was going better than either she or Matt had expected. More than half of the guests invited to the original retreat were able to attend, despite the short notice. They'd expanded the guest list to tastemakers and change agents in other industries. People like Chase Stratton and Dixon Benedict, both of whom had finally arrived and were seated in the auditorium.

After a quick update from Corinne and two other

members of her team, Teresa's next stop was the kitchen. She consulted with the chef on the gala dinner menu. They also reviewed all of the special meal requests of various guests. It seemed that nearly a third of the attendees had dietary restrictions, but the chef and his staff had everything well in hand.

Chef Riad offered to prepare her a lovely pasta and chicken dish so she could have a quick, early lunch. It would probably be her only chance to grab a bite until later that evening.

Since it was such a gorgeous day, he suggested that she enjoy her lunch on the patio beside the pool, where he'd have it delivered.

It was the perfect suggestion. She could get a little sun, enjoy the gardens and inspect the pool to ensure that everything was as it should be. As she approached the large heated outdoor art deco pool, Liam emerged from beneath the water.

She nearly dropped her cell phone at the sight of him.

The man is a ridiculously perfect physical specimen.

He strode in her direction, his lips pressed into a subtle smirk. The black Versace swim trunks he wore were imprinted with a gold Barocco scroll print and the iconic Greek key print at the waist. The length of Liam's swim shorts showed off his strong thighs, while the band at the waist highlighted his firm abs.

Liam ran his fingers through his dark hair, plastered to his head. His light blue eyes beamed in the sunlight.

"Good morning," he said finally, obviously pleased by her reaction to his barely clad body.

A tingle of electricity ran down her spine and she involuntarily sank her teeth into her lower lip. Thoughts of when she'd last seen him wearing that little filled her brain, and her body ached for him.

Damn him.

"Good morning," she stammered. *Get a hold of yourself, girl.* "The Sasha Project announcement went well."

"It was great to finally make it public. But as soon as we were done I needed to clear my head. So I went for a swim." He accepted two towels from the pool attendant and thanked her.

Liam wrapped one towel around his waist and hung the other around his neck, drying his hair.

"You know Nicolette Ryan, don't you?" Liam nodded toward a beautiful woman stretched out on a lounger beside the pool with her bare legs crossed.

Liam collapsed on the chair beside her and she offered him one of the two drinks that a poolside server had just delivered.

The muscles in Teresa's back and neck tensed. Her free hand clenched in a fist at her side.

Nicolette Ryan. The reporter. What the hell was Liam doing cozying up with her?

Had Liam been the one who'd leaked the photos and information about Teresa to the press? Was he playing some sick game to drive her away before she could liquidate her shares in Christopher Corporation?

"Good morning, Teresa." Nicolette waved cheerily. The woman's brown eyes sparkled and her dark hair was smoothed back into a low bun. Her creamy, light brown skin shone. "Thank you so much for granting me a press pass for this event. The grounds are remarkable and Jessie Humphrey's show last night was one of the best live performances I've ever experienced."

Teresa forced a smile, despite her tense shoulders. "Glad you could make the retreat on such short notice."

Nicolette gave her a knowing smile. "I wouldn't have missed it."

She lay back, stretched out in the warmth of the sun and closed her eyes.

Teresa gritted her teeth. She looked for a patio table that would allow her to eat in peace without seeing or hearing Liam and his new friend.

She plopped down in one of the wrought iron chairs at a patio table beneath a large umbrella and sulked.

No, she and Liam weren't a couple. And she had no right to dictate what activities he engaged in and with whom. Still, she couldn't help the churning in her gut, thinking of Nicolette and Liam doing God knows what together.

She cast a sideways glance in their direction. Heads together, they were engaged in a private conversation. One to which they obviously didn't want her to be privy. She could barely hear them whispering in hushed tones. For a moment, she regretted selecting a table so far away.

"Here you are, ma'am. Chef Riad's special chicken Alfredo, just for you." The server set down her plate and laid out her silverware. He poured a bottle of sparkling mineral water in her glass.

Teresa wished he'd shift just a little to the right so she could see exactly what Liam and Nicolette were doing.

Spying on Liam wouldn't help her sanity with all that was already going on. What she needed was distance.

"I'm sorry, but would you mind if I moved to the cabana the hotel gave us access to for the weekend?"

The server politely gathered everything up on his tray again before heading over to the cabana.

Once he was gone, Teresa ate her meal in peace, trying hard not to wonder about Liam or his newfound interest in the beautiful reporter.

"I feel terrible about the photos that leaked after the blackout at The Opulence." Nicolette Ryan sipped her piña colada. "And those awful headlines. They weren't fair to you or Teresa." She nodded toward the woman who'd moved to the other end of the pool.

Without turning his head, Liam glanced in Teresa's direction in time to see her get out of her seat and follow the server to one of the more secluded cabanas.

"Liam." Nicolette called his name impatiently, as if it wasn't the first time she'd had to say it.

"Yes, I'm sorry. I was just…thinking." He took a gulp of his Manhattan. He turned to face her fully. "So you think someone has it out for me?"

"At this point, I'm not sure if their grudge is against you personally or against your father's company. It's even possible that Teresa is the real target of this cruel game someone is playing."

Liam frowned, glanced involuntarily over his shoulder at the cabana that Teresa occupied. If someone had it out for her…why? Had she done something questionable in her past that would make someone want revenge? If so, just how far would they go to make her pay?

"Teresa could be in danger."

"I don't know." Nicolette shrugged. "But I'd suggest that you both operate on the side of caution. Someone has definitely been asking around about the two of you and inquiring about her history with your father."

Nicolette adjusted her lounger, sitting upright. "People often discount me because of the topics I cover. Celebrities, fashion, Hollywood and society gossip," she said bitterly. "But I operate with integrity. *Always*. I don't want to see you or Teresa get hurt. Nor do I want to see either of your reputations ruined. Watch out for unscrupulous reporters and paparazzi. They're like sharks, circling in the water, sniffing out blood."

"Who has been asking about me and about my father? If you know that someone is asking, surely you know who it is."

"I don't have all of the details." She shifted her gaze from his and sipped her drink.

"There's something you know, but aren't telling me." Liam studied Nicolette's face.

Her brown eyes wouldn't meet his. "I have to protect my sources. I've already told you too much. In fact, I'd better go and get ready for lunch. Mr. Richmond doesn't want his guests hounded by the press this weekend, but a few have agreed to talk to me. I have some interviews lined up."

"Wait, Nicolette." Liam placed a hand on her arm. "Surely there is something else you can tell me."

Nicolette scanned the space before returning her gaze to his. "I'm not one hundred percent sure who is behind this, but it's quite possible that the source is much closer to you than you think. If I were you, I'd be careful about who I trust."

"I will." Liam ran a hand through his damp hair. "Thank you for sharing what you could."

Nicolette slid on her shades, gathered her things and headed inside the hotel.

A source close to him?

The number of people he could trust not to keep secrets from him steadily decreased, starting with his parents. His father had pulled the rug from underneath him by leaving Teresa 25 percent of Christopher Corporation stock. Then there was the even bigger secret...

When Linus Christopher lay dying in the hospital, Liam had caught a glimpse of his father's medical records. Linus's blood type was listed as AB. He hadn't given it much thought at the time. But later it occurred to him that his own blood type was O. If the information in his father's chart was accurate, there was no way Linus Christopher was his father.

Parents were often hesitant to reveal to their children that they were adopted. But he wasn't a child. He was a thirty-two-year-old man who needed to know his medical history. So if he was adopted, why hadn't his parents told him the truth?

After his father's funeral, Liam had asked his mother, Catherine, about the discrepancy. She insisted the hospital chart had been mistaken. And she assured him he was their biological son.

Still, he couldn't stop thinking about it.

Maybe his mother was right and the admitting staff had made an egregious error. But then there was the emotional distance he'd always felt between himself and his father. It had never made sense to Liam. But if the medical chart was to be believed, his father's resentment suddenly made sense.

Then his father had gone and left a quarter of the company's shares to Teresa—a virtual stranger. It only fueled his suspicion that he may not be a Christopher after all.

Seventeen

The Richmond Industries fifth anniversary event was going off without a hitch. The accommodations and food were fantastic. The guests were all well-behaved and seemed to really be enjoying the experience. And the hotel staff's customer service was unparalleled. Teresa couldn't have asked for anything more.

Liam had been a genius for suggesting this venue and a saint for using his pull to secure the hotel for her on such short notice.

Teresa closed her eyes against the memory of Liam and Nicolette whispering together beside the pool. Despite her growing affection for the man, he didn't trust her, and without that, they had no future.

She needed to get her head in the game and focus on her work at Limitless Events and the Christopher

Corporation. That should be enough to keep her busy so she didn't think about Liam or how incredible his body had looked dripping wet.

Her phone buzzed. She lifted it and checked the new text message.

Speak of the devil.

Urgent. Meet me in my cottage in ten minutes. Need to speak with you in private.

Teresa frowned. Why couldn't Liam have asked her to meet him at the bar or even beside the pool?

Because none of those areas offered true privacy. And from the sound of his urgent text, the issue was sensitive and meant only for her ears. Still, going to see Liam Christopher in his cottage was a profoundly bad idea.

Teresa dialed Liam's phone, but the call rang until it went to his voice mail. She called it twice more and got the same.

Teresa frowned and tucked her hair behind her ear as she made another sweep of the lobby to ensure everything was fine. She gave a few quick instructions to the staff setting up lunch in the banquet hall and followed up with Corinne and Evelyn Montague. Then she made her way across the property to Liam's cottage.

She knocked on the door, but there was no answer. Teresa knocked again, miffed that Liam had sent her such a cryptic text but now wasn't answering his phone or the door. She was just about to turn and leave when Liam answered.

"Sorry, I was in the shower. Got sidetracked by an unexpected call." He answered the door with a towel slung low on his waist. Droplets of water from the shower still covered his body. "Come in."

Liam stepped aside to allow her into the room, then he glanced around the courtyard.

"Liam, what's going on?" Teresa demanded, her arms folded. "Were you checking to see if I was being followed?"

"Yes." He took the towel draped around his neck and dried his hair.

"By whom?"

"That's what I'd like to know." He went into the kitchen and pulled out a bottle of water, offering her one.

"No, thank you." Teresa went to the window and peeked outside. She pulled the curtains closed once she was convinced no one was there.

The man was seriously making her paranoid.

"Then why would you think someone is following me? And what's up with the cryptic text? I have a million things going on right now. So spare me the drama and tell me what's happening."

Liam excused himself to go into the bathroom and change, leaving her to pace in the living space, which opened to the bedroom. She found herself staring at the bed. Thoughts of the nights they'd shared filled her brain. For one happy moment she had truly believed that they could have something more. Something real.

But there was so much baggage between them. Her history with his father. Liam's inability to trust people, ingrained in him by his mother. The terms of his father's will and the suspicion and animosity that had created between them. The rumors that threatened both of their reputations and her livelihood.

"Is everything all right?" Liam placed a gentle hand on her arm, startling her. She hadn't even realized that he'd emerged from the bathroom. "I called you a couple of times but you were in a daze."

"I'm just running everything about tonight's gala through my head. Trying to make sure I didn't forget anything." There were enough secrets between them. She hated adding an inconsequential lie to the mix. "So you were going to explain the text."

"Right." He stepped away, creating space between them. As if he needed it as much as she did. "You might've noticed that I had a chance to chat with Nicolette Ryan, the lifestyle reporter for—"

"I know who Nicolette Ryan is, Liam." She folded her arms, her jaw tight. "I issued her press pass."

"Yes, of course," he conceded with a little smirk. He seemed to be getting a kick out of her spurned-lover routine. "The reason Nicolette wanted to speak to me so urgently was because she wanted to warn me...*us*, really."

"About?" Teresa raised an eyebrow.

"Nicolette doesn't believe that the leaking of those photos and videos of us was just some random act by someone trying to make a buck." Liam sat on the white sofa. "She thinks that someone has a calculated agenda to destroy one of us."

"Or perhaps both." Teresa sank onto the other end of the sofa and turned to him. "But who and why?"

"That's what we need to put our heads together and figure out," he said. "And soon. Preferably before they strike again and do more damage to our reputations and organizations. Christopher Corporation can easily ride out the current scandal, but if something else like this happens…"

"Limitless Events will be dead in the water." Teresa raised her eyes to his. "What do we do? I've invested everything I own in this company. I can't afford for it to fail. Too many people are counting on me. My staff, my family…"

"I know." Liam placed his large hand over hers, resting on the sofa between them. "And I'll do everything in my power to help keep that from happening. I hope you believe that."

Teresa nodded. "I do. You've already done so much. Getting Jessie Humphrey to The Opulence despite the weather. Getting this place for us on such short notice. You didn't have to do any of that."

Liam gave her a reluctant nod. He stood, pacing the floor. "We both need to be aware that there are unethical reporters out there who'd do anything to get a big story and some of them don't give a damn about the facts. They just want a juicy, salacious story, regardless of how fictitious it might be. I'm sure that people like that would think nothing of employing spies to get dirt on us or our companies. Perhaps even people we know and trust." He stared at her pointedly.

"You think there's a spy in my camp? Like one of my employees?" Teresa was incensed by Liam's suggestion. "I handpicked each and every member of my team. I'd vouch for any of them."

"I get it. They're good people. Seemingly trustworthy. But people aren't always who they seem."

"Like the fact that I'm not the home-wrecking gold digger you believed me to be?" She folded her arms, one brow raised. "Or that you're not the ogre I once thought you were?"

"Yes, people can surprise you for the better," Liam admitted. "But they can also stun you in truly terrible ways. We can't discount the probability of that."

Teresa stood, too. "Why do you automatically assume it's someone from my company? It could just as easily be someone from Christopher Corporation."

"True." He nodded sagely. "But aside from Duncan, I don't have a relationship with my employees that's quite as familiar as the one you have with yours. There's some truth to the saying that familiarity breeds contempt." He rubbed his jaw.

Teresa shook her head vehemently. "I still don't believe it. Besides, why would they do something that's jeopardizing their livelihood? I can see the fear in their eyes, Liam. They're all just as concerned as I am about the impact these rumors will have on the future of the company. I'm telling you, no one at Limitless Events would've done this. *No one*," she said again for emphasis.

Liam didn't try to hide his exasperation over her

unwillingness to believe one of her employees had sold her out for a quick payday.

"Maybe they are really honest, loyal, hardworking individuals." Liam focused his gaze on hers. "But if someone has an agenda against one of us, it's possible they'd stop at nothing to achieve their end. Even if it meant blackmailing someone close to us. Perhaps even threatening to harm a member of their family."

"Joshua…" Teresa pressed a hand to her forehead.

"You think your brother might've been compromised?" Liam asked. "Could that be why he went missing when you got that crank call about him?"

When she'd gotten a mysterious call implying that her brother may have been kidnapped, she'd confided that to Liam. He'd offered to have his investigator check into it and it turned out to be a hoax.

"Josh would never do anything to hurt me. Certainly nothing like this." Teresa didn't believe for a minute that her brother would be party to destroying her career. "Besides, he doesn't know about us. We haven't spoken in a while, and I certainly wouldn't tell my little brother that you and I…" Her eyes darted involuntarily to the bed in the other room. "It just couldn't be him, that's all."

Teresa paced the floor, her back to him. As soon as she left Liam's cottage, she needed to call her brother.

"Okay, if we can't figure out who, let's approach the other side of this."

"Which is?" Teresa turned back to Liam, studying his face.

He ran his hands through his dark hair and his expression offered an unspoken apology. "I need you to be completely honest with me, Teresa. Is there more to the story about what happened between you and my father? Are there any more stories that are likely to come out?"

It hurt that Liam felt the need to ask the question again. That he still didn't fully believe her though she'd told him the unvarnished truth. She was never romantically involved with his father. Linus Christopher had been nothing more than a friend and mentor to her.

"How many times and how many ways do I have to say it?" she seethed. "I did *not* have an affair with your father. I wouldn't. And I never saw him as anything other than a mentor. I hadn't seen Linus in years. I'm as shocked as you are that he'd leave me twenty-five percent of the company."

Liam grimaced when she mentioned the portion of the company she held. "I believe you about my father," he said quietly. He didn't want to ask about her father's connection to Christopher Corporation until Dutton gave him more to go on. "But is there anything else you might have to worry about? Anything that might cause a problem for your company or mine? Because, as you indicated, you now own a quarter of the company. So it's not just Limitless that's in jeopardy."

"I do have secrets." She shrugged. "Doesn't everyone?"

Liam stepped closer. "But is there anything that could be damaging to the reputation of Christopher Corporation?"

"I already told you about my brother and his problems. That he got in trouble with some dangerous people in Vegas and owed them a lot of money."

"The trouble that the Fixer helped you get him out of." Liam folded his arms and frowned. "It isn't ideal, of course. But we could probably find a way to spin the story. Everyone loves the story of a person who would go to bat for their family, at all costs."

"It isn't a story, Liam. It's the truth. Maybe this is all just about bad press to you, but this is my life." Her voice broke and tears burned her eyes. She swiped a finger beneath one eye, trying not to ruin her makeup. "Not that you'd understand."

"Teresa, wait…"

Before he could stop himself, Liam had caught her hand in his. She turned back to look at him. Hurt and disappointment filled the lovely blue eyes he'd found himself drowning in just a few short weeks ago.

"I realize how difficult this must all be for you. I didn't intend to come off as an insensitive, self-centered boor." He rubbed his thumb over the soft skin on the back of her hand. "I've been groomed my entire life to think of Christopher Corporation first and everything second…including the people in my life. I never much liked being on the receiving end of that treatment. That's something I need to remember going forward."

Teresa nodded, looking at him thoughtfully. The night the tree crashed on top of her, he'd told her about the rocky relationship he'd had with his parents. Had admitted how painful it was for him growing up. So he knew she understood what he meant. He appreciated the compassion in her eyes.

"There is one other thing I should tell you." She dropped her gaze from his momentarily. "The only reason I didn't reject your father's gift of shares in the company is because the man who made the threatening phone call about my brother implied that Joshua owed someone money. A lot of it."

"How much?"

"The caller said seven million dollars. I knew Joshua owed some money a long time ago, but I thought when the Fixer bailed Josh out, those debts were settled, too."

It was all starting to become clear to Liam. "So you'd like to have the money on hand, just in case."

"Yes." More tears rolled down her face and her cheeks turned crimson, as if she was embarrassed by showing emotion in front of him. She swiped at the tears angrily with her free hand.

"You didn't have to tell me that." Liam couldn't help staring at her firm, kissable lips. "Why did you?"

She looked at him squarely again. "Because I don't want there to be any secrets between us."

Liam cradled her cheek, wiping away her tears

with his thumb. He stepped closer to this beautiful woman who had an uncanny gift for making him feel an array of emotions. Anger, frustration, lust, jealousy, pain and a deep, growing affection that seemed to squeeze his chest whenever he thought of her.

He leaned in so slowly it felt as if he could hear the seconds ticking in his head. Teresa didn't object. Instead, she leaned closer, too. Her eyes drifted closed.

Liam pressed his mouth to hers and kissed her.

Teresa let go of his hand and relaxed into him, her hands pressed to his chest as she angled her head, giving him better access. He trailed kisses across her salty, tearstained cheeks. Then he pressed a soft kiss to her ear.

"Why is it that I can never resist kissing you?" he whispered.

"Maybe it's the same reason I can't help wanting you to kiss me." Her breathy reply did things to him. "Or stop thinking about the nights we spent together."

He kissed her again, and she parted her lips to him, inviting him to deepen the kiss. He obliged, his tongue gliding against hers. He reveled in the sweet, minty taste of her warm mouth.

The kiss that had started off slow and tentative escalated. The hunger in his kiss was matched by the eagerness in hers.

Her arms snaked around his waist, and her fingers pressed into his back, pulling their bodies closer. He wanted her. Hadn't been able to stop thinking about her. And he'd used nearly every excuse he could manufacture to spend time with her.

Everything he'd been taught from the time he was a boy told him he shouldn't trust her. That he should resent her intrusion into his life and the way she'd insinuated herself into his family's business.

But another part of him found Teresa to be a breath of fresh air in a world filled with self-important blowhards whose bank accounts were the most interesting thing about them.

She made him feel things he hadn't felt before. Things he wanted to feel again. So despite the promise he'd made to himself, he wanted to taste her skin. To experience the passion they'd shared as they brought each other mind-blowing pleasure.

Liam broke their kiss, his eyes searching hers for permission. Teresa sank her teeth into her bottom lip, her breathing ragged as she removed her suit jacket and tossed it over the chair. She turned her back to him, giving him access to the zipper of her bustier.

He leaned in and pressed a soft kiss to her neck and shoulder as he unzipped the fabric, threaded with a metallic silver. He tossed it on top of her suit jacket in the chair. His hands glided up her belly as he kissed her shoulders. He palmed her breasts.

Teresa whimpered. Her knees buckled slightly and her curvy bottom pressed against him. He slid the zipper down the side of her slim gray pants. She kicked off her heels, standing in her bare feet and a silvery gray lace thong.

He turned her around, pressing another kiss to her mouth as he lifted her. She wrapped her lean legs around him as he carried her to the bed.

Liam stripped off his clothing, thankful the boutique hotel provided a welcome kit that included a handful of little foil packets. He sheathed himself, then tugged off the little scrap of lace and dropped it to the floor.

He kissed her. Savored the sensation as her body welcomed his. Her fingers dug into his back as he drove deep inside her. Their bodies moved together. Their murmurs of pleasure growing more intense as they each hurtled closer to their edge.

Teresa froze, her fingernails scraping his skin as she called his name. The contraction of the muscles deep in her core sent ripples of pleasure up his spine that brought him over the edge.

He cursed, his body trembling as he collapsed on the bed beside her, struggling to catch his breath.

Neither of them spoke.

Finally, he rolled over and propped his fist beneath his head as he lay facing her. He trailed a hand down her stomach. "That was…" He blew out a breath, words escaping him.

A smile lit her eyes. "It was, wasn't it?"

"It always is between us."

Teresa's phone rang. She glanced at the clock on the wall, then cursed beneath her breath and climbed out of bed.

"I have to get back." She gathered her clothing.

"Of course, but do you have to go this instant?" He hoped for an encore as soon as he recovered.

"Yes." She rushed into the bathroom, but smiled over her shoulder at him. "But I'll take a rain check for later tonight."

He grinned, already counting the minutes.

Eighteen

Teresa smoothed the gorgeous blue floor-length Zac Posen fishtail gown she'd gotten for a steal down over her hips. She took one last look in the mirror as she carefully applied her matte red Dior lipstick. Then she dropped the tube in her clutch.

Today had been hectic. She'd handled several last-minute preparations, headed off potential problems and resolved a few unusual guest requests. But there were two events that had shaken her the most during the course of the day. Learning that someone may be acting on a calculated vendetta against her and…

Teresa's body tingled with electricity as it seemed to relive the trail that Liam's strong hand had taken as it moved across her skin. She'd allowed herself to be pulled under again by her attraction to him.

Not just because he was an incredibly sexy man. Though her eyes drifted closed briefly at the memory of Liam emerging from the pool in those swim shorts. She was attracted to him because, despite the distrust and bravado, at his core he was a sweet and thoughtful man. He'd come to her aid in countless ways in the past few months. Many of which he hadn't even wanted her to know about. He'd done it simply because she needed the help.

Still, were their physical attraction, similar interests and the fact that they enjoyed spending time together enough to overcome Liam's issues with trust and the nasty rumors out there about her?

Teresa pushed the disquieting thoughts from her mind. She had a gala to manage. And tonight would go off without a hitch.

She'd do whatever was necessary to ensure it.

"Teresa."

Matt approached with Nadia on his arm.

Teresa had brought Nadia on at Limitless Events as a contractor when it became evident that she wouldn't be able to keep her job as Matt's assistant once they became involved. She was smart, resourceful, hardworking and trustworthy. Which made her the perfect fit. But this was her husband's event, so Nadia was a client, too, serving as Matt's official cohost.

Nadia looked gorgeous in a strapless red gown with her blonde hair twisted in an elaborate updo. And despite his disdain for suits, the man wore an athletic-fit tuxedo that highlighted his muscular physique.

"This weekend has been fabulous. A wonderful way to celebrate Richmond Industries' fifth anniversary. It was a great call having the retreat here. Almost makes the disaster we endured last month worthwhile." He chuckled, his arm wrapped around Nadia's waist.

"It truly has been a wonderful weekend." Nadia's gaze met Matt's.

Her brown eyes glinted in the light and her cheeks flushed as her husband drank her in. As if he were seeing her for the very first time.

"You've honestly outdone yourself, Teresa." Nadia finally turned to meet her gaze. "Thank you for all of your hard work. With such short notice for the re-scheduled event, I know it wasn't easy. Quite frankly, this was something of a miracle. Far more than we expected, given the timeline."

She nudged Matt, who was looking at Nadia dreamily once again.

"You've done outstanding work, Teresa. We'll be in touch to discuss the plans for our next retreat."

Matt excused himself and he and Nadia walked away to greet their guests.

Teresa was thrilled that Matt was so pleased. Just a few more hours and she could put this event in the books as a phenomenal success.

"Teresa St. Claire, I'm Brooks Abbingdon." A tall, handsome man with curly hair approached her. His wide smile gleamed. "We don't know each other, but—"

"Of course I know who you are, Mr. Abbingdon." Teresa smiled. "You're the CEO of Abbingdon Airlines, one of the fastest-growing private airline companies in the country." She shook the hand he'd extended.

"And you're the woman who put this incredible event together in just two weeks." Brooks grinned.

He was handsome with creamy, light brown skin. His dark hair had a natural curl and he towered over her at well over six feet in height. His liquid brown eyes and gleaming broad smile were simply mesmerizing. No wonder the man had a reputation as something of a playboy.

"I didn't do it alone, of course. I have an incredible staff." Teresa could barely contain her smile. After what she'd been through these past few months, it felt good to have everything going so smoothly and to receive such heartfelt acknowledgment from Matt Richmond and now Brooks Abbingdon, one of his high-powered guests.

"I'm sure you still have lots to do tonight, Ms. St. Claire, so I won't take up too much of your time." Brooks stepped closer and lowered his voice. "I'd like to discuss the possibility of engaging your services for an upcoming event."

"Call me Teresa." Her belly fluttered with excitement. A new, high-profile client like Brooks Abbingdon was *exactly* what Limitless Events needed right now. The success of the Richmond retreat and being tasked with planning an event for the popular bachelor could be just the thing to pull her company out of the sharp decline that began because of the recent scandal. "Thank you for considering Limitless Events. May I ask what kind of event you're planning?"

He grinned and his eyes, the color of dark, rich coffee, twinkled. "My wedding."

"Congratulations! I didn't realize you were engaged."

Teresa liked to keep up with the latest on the wealthy and powerful of Seattle. Especially when the news meant that they might need her services.

"I'd be honored to work with you to plan your wedding. If you give me the basics—your fiancée's name, the time of year you'd like to get married, the date, if you've set one, and any ideas you have about your ideal wedding—my assistant will work up some preliminary ideas to present to you when we get together."

Teresa pulled out her phone and started typing an email to Corinne.

"I appreciate your enthusiasm," Brooks said. "But I realize how busy your team must be. This is Matt's event, so I won't impose on his time, but I'll definitely be in touch."

Brooks flashed his megawatt smile and walked away before she could object. He was headed right for Nicolette Ryan, who had set up in a lovely area of the hotel lobby to interview some of the guests as background for her coverage of the retreat.

Not surprising.

The man could teach a master class on how to manipulate the press to one's advantage and have them love you for it.

Besides, he was right. She had a million things to keep watch over, beginning with making sure that Jessie had arrived in the staging area and would be ready to perform in less than an hour.

Liam stood by the bar and watched couples swaying on the dance floor to a big band song the musicians were playing. The retreat had been outstanding, and the announcement of the Sasha Project that morning had gone well, but the Saturday night gala was simply phenomenal.

The decor was modern glitz and glamour that played upon the Old Hollywood feel of the hotel's art deco style. And hiring a group to play big band songs and Rat Pack standards was a stroke of genius.

The food Chef Riad prepared had surpassed his expectations and The Goblet's private-label wine produced at the on-site vineyard was one of the best cabernets he'd ever had. It was so good that he'd forgone his usual Manhattan for the evening.

Liam caught a glimpse of Teresa as she darted through the crowd in search of the next fire to be put out. He wasn't sure how, but the woman seemed to get more gorgeous each time he laid eyes on her.

The stunning blue dress she wore complemented the color of her eyes and fit her body like a glove. It was sleeveless with a low neckline, so it showcased her strong arms and provided just enough cleavage to make his imagination go wild.

Only he didn't need imagination. He'd seen the full show and it was spectacular. Memories of that body haunted him in the middle of the night when he lay in bed alone, wishing she were there beside him.

Satisfaction washed over him when his gaze met Teresa's from across the room. Her eyes danced and a soft, sexy grin curved one corner of her mouth.

It took every bit of self-control he could manage to stay rooted in place when what he wanted more than anything was to pull her into his arms and kiss her. To remind her of what they'd shared earlier in the day when he'd made love to her in his cottage.

In fact, as wonderful as the event had been, he couldn't wait until it was over so he could take her back to his room and have her again.

"She looks amazing in that dress, doesn't she?" Nadia stood beside Liam. They both stared at Teresa as she dealt with one of the other guests.

"She does." Liam sipped from his wineglass and kept his response even. "As do you in yours." He nodded toward his friend's wife. "And nearly every other woman in this room, for that matter."

"Yes, but you are not staring at me or any other woman in this room." Nadia gave him a knowing grin. "You're staring at one woman in particular. And it seems that she is quite taken with you, too." Nadia cocked her head, watching Teresa for a moment. Suddenly the woman's eyes lit up. "Why don't you ask her to dance?"

"She's working and I—"

"The party is pretty much under control, and I know for a fact Matt wouldn't mind. So ask her." Nadia nudged him. "If you don't, I have the feeling you're going to regret it."

The woman sashayed off in her strapless red gown with her blond hair twisted up. Nadia was a beautiful woman and his best friend was a lucky man.

Perhaps she was onto something with her suggestion.

Liam finished the last of his wine and made his way to where Teresa stood near the back of the room monitoring the gala.

"You look stunning." He stood beside her, both of them watching the band on the stage. Liam placed a discreet hand low on her back and whispered in her ear. "But I happen to know for a fact that you'd look even better out of it."

Her cheeks flushed and she grinned. "You look pretty good yourself." She gave him a quick, sideways glance. Her grin deepened. "In or out of the tux."

Teresa surveyed the crowd, as if she was worried about who might be watching the two of them together.

Liam hated that it had come to this between them. They both needed to protect their business interests and their reputations. He realized that. But by allowing some shadowy figure to control their actions, they were giving the person power over them. Emboldening him to do who knew what next.

On the other hand, if they behaved as if the rumors had no effect on them, perhaps the culprit would realize he hadn't succeeded and just move on.

"I'd better go," Teresa said, pulling away from him.

He tightened his grip on her waist. "Don't. At least, not yet."

"Why not?" She turned to face him, a look of panic in her eyes.

The band played the opening chords of Frank Sinatra's "The Way You Look Tonight" and Liam smiled.

Perfect.

He removed his hand from her waist and extended it to her. "Dance with me."

"What?" She looked at him as if he'd lost his mind. "You want me to dance with you? Here? Where everyone can see us?"

"Yes to all of the above." He smiled. "This is my favorite song, and I can't think of anyone I'd rather dance to it with tonight."

"That's sweet, Liam." Her expression softened into a dreamy smile for a moment, but then she glanced over to the spot where Matt and Nadia stood. "But aside from all of the other reasons it isn't good for us to be seen dancing together, I'm working, remember?"

"Let me worry about Matt, okay?" He nodded toward the dance floor. "Come on. Just one dance. That's all I'm asking."

"One dance." She slipped her hand in his. "But

don't expect me to kiss you in the middle of the dance floor this time."

Liam burst into laughter, remembering when Teresa kissed him for the first time on the dance floor at Gideon John's party. It had been completely unexpected, but not unwelcome. He'd gladly kissed her back.

"Well, you never know. Maybe I'll kiss you this time."

They found a place on the dance floor not far from where they'd been standing. He took her in his arms and swayed to the music, singing along softly so only she could hear.

It felt right to hold her like this. To stop hiding and pretending that he didn't care for this woman as much as he did. It was obvious that they couldn't stay away from each other, no matter how hard either of them tried. So maybe they should stop fighting the growing feeling between them.

What was the worst that could happen if they just admitted that what they felt for each other was more than either of them had expected? That it was powerful and intense and worth exploring more fully, rumors be damned?

"This is one of my favorite songs, too." She tipped her chin to look up at him. There was a mixture of happiness and sorrow in her glistening eyes. "My mother listened to it when I was a kid. She and my dad danced to this song the first night they met. She plays it often, particularly when she's really missing my father."

"I'm sorry, sweetheart." He stopped singing and swaying to the music. "I didn't mean to make you sad."

"You didn't." She widened her smile and swiped the dampness from her eyes. "I hadn't heard the song in a long time. And I've never been serenaded with it before. It just struck me because…well, my mother always told the story of how my dad did the same thing the night they met. It just made me a little nostalgic."

"Happy memories, then?" Liam stared into her eyes, fighting the overwhelming desire to kiss her.

He wanted to articulate all of the feelings for her he'd been struggling with. But Teresa was here in a professional capacity, and he needed to respect that. Even if his body didn't.

"Happy-ish." She forced a smile.

"You haven't said much about your father," Liam noted, taking her in his arms again and slowly swaying.

"I guess I haven't. It's not something I talk about very—" Her phone rang and she gave him an apologetic frown. "I'm sorry, Liam, but I need to take this."

"Of course. You're working." He released her from his grip and shoved a hand in his pocket. "I understand."

She pulled the phone from her purse and read the screen. "It's Evelyn Montague. I'd better see what she wants. Besides, there are a few things I need to confirm about the farewell breakfast tomorrow morning. I have to go, but we're still on for later, right?"

"Nothing could possibly keep me away." Liam grinned. "I'll see you then."

Liam hated that Teresa had to go, but he thoroughly enjoyed the view as she sashayed across the room in that fitted blue gown, the fishtail hem swishing in her wake.

His body ached for this vibrant, brilliant, beautiful woman. In his head, they were already back in that cottage where his biggest problem would be finding the zipper so he could strip her out of that dress.

Liam went to the bar to order himself a Manhattan. As he sipped his cocktail, he silently assessed the crowd.

He felt secure in his decision not to allow the coward hiding in the shadows to dictate his life. But a small part of him hoped like hell he hadn't just thrown gasoline on the fire by pissing off whoever had an ax to grind with either him or Teresa.

Nineteen

Jessie paced the greenroom as she warmed up her voice and reviewed the final changes she'd made to both the lyrics and the musical arrangement of the song she'd be singing for the audience. Tonight's performance had to be absolutely perfect.

Teresa had confirmed that both Chase Stratton and Dixon Benedict were out in the crowd mingling. Dixon had even mentioned to Teresa that he was eager to hear Jessie perform live. In addition to the two dream producers for her project being in the audience, Teresa had informed her that entertainment reporter Nicolette Ryan would be broadcasting her performance live from her show's website and social media pages.

The live broadcast meant that tonight's performance had the potential to either be a viral sensation or a hot, flaming mess that could spawn a dozen memes and make her an industry joke.

Jessie preferred to believe it would be the former, not the latter. She just needed to showcase her songwriting and voice together in a way the syrupy pop album hadn't permitted her to.

Even if Chase and Dix passed on her project, maybe the live broadcast would capture the interest of another producer on her top ten list.

No. Don't think that way.

Jessie released a deep breath to drain the tension from her body. Tension in her jaw, chest and throat would make her voice tight and strained. In the bigger moments of the song, she'd sound like she was trying too hard instead of singing from deep down in the bottom of her soul. So she had to relax. Let go of all of her anxiety about the big moment ahead.

She smoothed her hands down the ethereal one-shoulder floor-length Laylahni Couture gown. Jessie had fallen in love with the dress the moment she'd laid eyes on it. She loved the contrast of the pale pink silk chiffon against her warm brown skin. And there was something so Old Hollywood about the twisted tulle overlay, embroidered skirt and bodice, and short but elegant train.

The gown made her feel beautiful, but also strong. She was a woman who was completely in control of her destiny. All she had to do was give an honest, raw performance. Leave it all out there on that stage for everyone to see.

Jessie continued her vocal exercises and warmed up her wrists and fingers.

With her entire future riding on this performance, Jessie tried not to think about Gideon being in the audience. Nearly impossible since her brain had been flooded with thoughts of Gideon all day. She couldn't help wondering how he felt about her and whether he was truly over her sister.

A mood which matched the raw, personal song she was unveiling tonight. "Okay" explored the pain of being in love with a person who loves someone else.

She wasn't a starry-eyed teen anymore and she now had a renewed understanding of their past. So why did this song still sum up exactly how she was feeling? And how would she react to singing those words with Gideon just a few yards away?

Lean into it. Use it as fuel.

Jessie drilled the words in her head again and again. She tried to release the apprehension rising in her stomach. To ignore the lingering feelings for the man who clearly still wasn't over her sister.

No matter how deeply she'd buried her feelings for Gideon over the years, they kept resurfacing. Maybe it was the same for Gideon where Geneva was concerned.

Even if he did have feelings for her, what did she expect to come of it? He had his life back in Seattle and she had hers in New York. She'd seen what happened to other female artists when they'd gotten serious about a rich and powerful man. It meant the death of their careers. And when the relationship was over, and it inevitably was, the woman was left to resurrect her career from the smoldering ashes.

That wasn't the fate Jessie wanted for herself.

Choosing Gideon meant *not* choosing her career. A career she'd worked for her entire adult life. One she wouldn't walk away from just because she'd reunited with her old crush.

Gideon had moved from his table near the stage and taken a seat at the bar at the back of the room. He didn't want to be a distraction to Jessie. He understood how much was at stake.

He sipped the whiskey he'd ordered neat. Gideon welcomed the heat building in his chest as the smooth liquor with a fiery bite washed down his throat. It'd been fifteen years since that incident with Jessie, and the shock of her kissing him felt as fresh now as it had then. But now he found himself in a completely new dilemma.

He felt something for Jessie. Something deeper than friendship or physical attraction. Something he wanted to explore. Yet the prospect of getting involved with his ex's sister gave him pause.

How would Geneva react to him and Jessie being together?

The last thing he wanted to do was cause animosity between the sisters. Nor did he want anyone to think this was some sick attempt to get back at his ex.

And what if things did work out between him and Jessie? He'd have to find a way to let go of his resentment of her parents.

Gideon took another swig of his whiskey. He should be celebrating right now, not agonizing over his feelings for Jessie.

Despite all of the drama, they'd secured the remaining funding for the project in Dubai and managed to pull the deal off. Construction would begin on time.

This was when he normally celebrated with a perfectly aged bottle of bourbon and the warmth and comfort of a beautiful stranger. But he hadn't looked at another woman since he'd laid eyes on Jessie.

It had driven him crazy to watch the men here fawning all over her last night. Most of them had no real interest in her other than the bragging rights of having slept with a celebrity.

He'd wanted to tell her last night that the tables had turned. That it was him who desperately wanted her. For a moment when they'd danced together, he believed she wanted the same thing. That she would be open to spending the evening with him, even if all they did was catch up on each other's lives.

But then Jessie had started asking questions about Geneva. Fishing to see if he had any lingering feelings for her sister. He'd answered her questions honestly. That included admitting he'd gone to Zurich ten years ago with hopes of rekindling what he'd thought they once had.

The evening had quickly gone off the rails from there.

After Jessie's performance, he would tell her the truth. Geneva had been his first love, so he'd held on to a romanticized view of their relationship. But they'd been too different from the start, and those differences had expanded over the course of their relationship. He'd tried to hold on to her by asking her to marry him.

It would've been a mistake.

One that would've left them both miserable and resentful. Altered the course of his life in ways he didn't want to imagine. He and Geneva were both exactly where they should be. And he was convinced that Jessie's reappearing at this point in his life was meant to be, too.

It would be a mistake to dismiss what he and Jessie were feeling just to spare Geneva's feelings when she was more than five thousand miles away.

Now if only he could convince Jessie of the same.

They announced Jessie's name and she emerged onstage to the sound of thunderous applause, aided by the fabulous acoustics in the room.

The sight of this woman, more beautiful than he could have ever imagined, stole his breath away.

Jessie wore an exquisite rose-colored gown worthy of anyone's red carpet. The goddess-style gown had a sheer overlay that covered one shoulder and added an elegant dimension to the dress. The fabric hugged her hips and dropped straight to the floor, but formed a short, graceful train behind her. And the dusty pink color popped nicely against Jessie's flawless brown skin.

She wore her dark brown natural hair in loose ringlets that dusted her shoulders. She'd captured the attention of everyone in the room and she hadn't even opened her mouth.

Jessie took a seat at the piano, adjusted the microphone and greeted the crowd. She went right into one of the songs from her recent pop album. But not one of the ones that got frequent airplay. It was a soulful tune about the highs and lows of being in love called "Nobody But You." As she sang about a love that, even in the tough times, was better than the best times with someone else, he couldn't help wondering who'd inspired that song.

Whomever it had been, Gideon couldn't help feeling a twinge of jealousy. For the first time in a very long time, he yearned for that kind of relationship. The kind that made you eager to return home at the end of a long, busy day because the person you loved was there waiting for you.

Jessie played the crescendo of the song, and the pounding of the keys brought him out of the daze he'd gone into. If he was looking for someone who'd be waiting for him at the end of a long, hard day, he'd set his sights on the wrong woman. He was in Seattle and she was in New York.

Gideon owned properties in New York, Miami and Los Angeles and on the beach in Costa Rica. Place wasn't the biggest challenge to exploring a relationship with Jessie. It was their careers.

He'd be making frequent trips to Dubai to oversee the deal and when the album was done, Jessie would undoubtedly spend several months out on tour.

How could they expect to make a life together when they wouldn't be on the same continent?

He was in a very different place in his life now. This weekend, he'd been quietly observing the joy and contentment of men like Matt Richmond. No longer moving from one conquest to the next, Matt seemed genuinely happy.

And for the first time in his life, as he watched the men around him on the hunt, he recognized the faint emptiness in their pursuits. Something he'd long felt deep down inside, though he'd always ignored it.

He'd focused on the high of the next big deal and the solitude at the bottom of a well-earned glass of whiskey. The temporary comfort and fleeting company offered by a pretty face.

He didn't want to live that way anymore.

Maybe it was because of Jessie. Or maybe it was a realization that had been a long time coming. Either way, he wouldn't let Jessie walk out of his life without telling her how he felt.

Gideon was mesmerized by her soulful performance. Her melodic voice had range. She was capable of going low with a voice that was gritty and raw. But she could also hit notes in her upper range that were simply angelic. Her lyrics touched him in a way no performance ever had.

He watched her onstage, completely rapt by her performance, like nearly every other person in that room, including the two producers she was so eager to meet with.

"Thank you so much." Jessie seemed genuinely

shocked by the enthusiastic applause that just wouldn't die down after her last song. "You all have been such a wonderful audience. So I'd like to show you my appreciation by sharing a new song with you that I haven't performed for anyone else. It's called 'Okay,' and I hope you like it."

Gideon finished the last of his whiskey and set the glass down on the bar as he turned back to the stage. For the first time that night, Jessie's eyes met his as she sang the opening lines of the song.

"You were the only one I ever wanted. Your heart was the only one that spoke to mine. But it was never me that you wanted. You loved the one I stood behind."

Her words and the pain in her voice and in her eyes as she said them felt like a punch to the throat. But he couldn't look away, no matter how deeply the words cut.

She turned her attention to Chase and Dixon, who seemed just as rapt by Jessie's performance.

Jessie's voice was raw and powerful. You could almost hear a pin drop in the space as she performed the song.

Her eyes met his again as she sang the chorus. "You deserve to be happy, for that I'll be glad in time. Right now my heart is still aching, but just know I'm gonna be fine. Because I'm okay, okay. Even though my heart is still breaking. I'll be okay, okay. So for that, love, one day I'll thank you. Because I made it to the other side…okay."

He'd wanted to stand up at the back of the room

and tell her right there in front of everyone how damn sorry he was things worked out the way they did between them. That he hated that it took fifteen years for them to find each other again. That the time was right for a second chance for them.

Instead, he placed his hand over his heart, then blew her a kiss.

Her eyes widened and she acknowledged his gesture with a quick smile, the emotion in her voice intensifying. When she was done, the entire room erupted with applause and Dixon Benedict jumped to his feet. The rest of his table and the rest of the room quickly followed.

Tears glistened in Jessie's eyes. "Thank you all so much. This has been such a tremendous night and I just want to say…"

Suddenly Jessie froze, her eyes filled with fear as a man babbling incoherently made his way to the front. He hopped on the stage, swiped the microphone from Jessie's hand and started to yell into it, his speech slurred.

Gideon sprinted toward the stage as quickly as his legs would carry him.

Twenty

It felt like everything was moving in slow motion. Liam had been lost in thought as he listened to Jessie Humphrey sing about loving someone you wanted to be with, but couldn't. He didn't see the man until he'd already climbed onto the stage.

Next, he saw Gideon Johns rushing toward the stage, leaping over a chair or two to do so. Liam was closer, so he jumped into action. He climbed onto the stage and tackled the man, who was still mumbling incoherently about rich liars and losers.

The man thrashed wildly. His elbow nearly caught Liam in the chin. Liam punched the man, knocking him out cold.

Liam shook his throbbing right hand and tried to catch his breath. "Jessie, are you all right?"

"I'm fine." She nodded. "How about you?"

"Jessie!" Gideon rushed onto the stage and gripped her arms. "He didn't hurt you, did he?"

"No, not physically." She turned to watch as the crowd was escorted from the room by members of the security team Matt had hired for the event.

"Where the hell were you guys *before* this drunk party-crasher leaped onto the stage?" Liam barked at the men, who lowered their eyes and continued to evacuate the room.

Gideon pulled Jessie against him as he stared at the man lying unconscious on the floor. It was as if he was waiting for him to climb to his feet so he could land his own punch.

Two members of the security team climbed onto the stage to assess the crazed man.

Another approached Jessie. "Miss Humphrey, I need to escort you to your room until we've assessed the threat."

Jessie turned away from the man and stared up at Gideon, her eyes wide. The poor woman looked traumatized.

"No." Gideon hugged her against him tightly. "She's staying with me. I'll see that she's okay."

Jessie gave him a grateful half-smile, then confirmed to the man that she was staying with Gideon.

The security man walked away reluctantly, then noticed Nicolette Ryan's cameraman with his camera still propped on his shoulder. "Are you still filming?"

Nicolette, who'd been staring at the stage in horror, was shaken from her daze. She rushed over to her cameraman and placed her hand over the lens. "Cut it. Now!"

He shut off the camera and the two made their way toward the exit. Nicolette turned back and mouthed "Sorry" to Jessie.

"Get me out of here, please." Jessie clutched Gideon's chest as she turned her head away from where other guests were filming the ruckus on stage as they filed out of the room. "Now," she pleaded.

"Have you got this under control?" Gideon asked Liam as he clutched Jessie, who'd buried her face in his chest.

"We're fine. Just take care of her." Liam wiggled his fingers, making sure none were broken.

"Thank you, Liam." Gideon shook his left hand, then escorted Jessie from the stage.

"I can't believe this." Teresa hurried toward the stage, going against the flow of the crowd. "I was in the kitchen speaking to Chef Riad when we heard screaming and people running. What on earth happened?"

"This dude crashed the party, climbed onto the stage and ripped the microphone out of Jessie's hand." Liam hopped down to the floor and pointed over his shoulder to the man still facedown on the stage. Liam shook his aching hand. "I had to sucker punch the guy before he hurt someone. He was behaving erratically, like he's on something major."

"Your hand is swelling." Teresa took his hand in hers gingerly and examined it. "We should get you to a doctor."

"I'll be fine." Liam shrugged. "I just need to submerge my hand in an ice bucket. Is there one around here somewhere?"

"At the bar, I'm sure. I'll take you back there and—" Teresa pressed a hand to her mouth and hurried onto the stage.

"Teresa, what's wrong?" Liam turned back to look at her.

She rushed toward the man the security guys had flipped onto his back. She dropped to her knees in her beautiful dress and hovered over him. Her hands were pressed to the floor on either side of the man's head.

"Josh, honey. It's me, Teresa. Are you okay?"

"Josh? As in your brother, Joshua St. Claire?" Liam stood in front of the stage.

"Yes." Teresa patted her brother's cheek, attempting to wake him. "I don't know what he's doing here or how he even knew where I'd be. We haven't spoken in weeks."

"Well, someone obviously told him where to find you." Matt Richmond approached them. He was clearly furious with Teresa. "How did this happen? You assured me that your personal issues wouldn't impact my event."

"It didn't, I mean I couldn't have known—" She stammered, her face red and her eyes brimming with tears. "I'm so sorry, Matt. I don't know how this happened, but I promise I'll find out."

"A lot of damn good that'll do me," he said bitterly.

"Take it easy, Matt." Liam held up his open palms. "I realize you're upset, but so is she." He gestured toward Teresa. "Your security team can sort out what happened later. I'll take care of this. Why don't you and Nadia go and try to calm the guests. Hopefully, everything will be back up and running soon."

"That's a good idea, Matt." Nadia squeezed his hand. "The guests need to see that you're calm and that this is just a minor inconvenience."

"Fine, but we will get to the bottom of this." Matt huffed, wrapping an arm around Nadia. "Your mother tried to warn me against using Limitless Events. I should've listened," he groused.

"My mother contacted you?" Liam turned to his friend.

Matt nodded. "Too bad I didn't listen."

Liam's mother still believed Teresa had had an affair with his father back when he mentored her as a college student. She hadn't been pleased that Liam no longer believed it. Still, he didn't think his mother would go out of her way to bash Teresa's business and hamper her ability to make a living.

"Will you be pressing charges against my brother?" Teresa asked quietly as she knelt beside Joshua. He was breathing normally, but still unconscious.

"I honestly don't know yet." Matt dragged a hand through his close-cropped hair in frustration. "Do you think Corinne and the rest of your staff can manage the remainder of the retreat without you?"

"Yes," Teresa stammered, her eyes wide.

"Good, because I want you and your brother out of here as soon as possible," Matt said.

Teresa nodded, tears streaming down her face.

Her career was over and her brother was in deep trouble. Even if Liam hadn't given him a serious concussion and Matt didn't press trespassing or assault charges against Josh, he had another problem. If anyone was looking for him, they might've seen him on the live internet broadcast. That meant they knew where he was.

She hadn't talked to him in weeks. Who knew what kind of trouble he might've gotten himself into this time?

Perhaps it was a good thing Matt wanted them to leave.

"Joshua," Teresa whispered, running her hands through her brother's dark hair to check for a bump. "What've you done now?"

"Teresa, I didn't realize this was your brother. Obviously, I wouldn't have hit the guy so hard if I'd known." Liam stood on the floor in front of the stage. A frown furrowed his brow.

She wasn't sure if it was because of the shitshow Joshua had just put on or because his hand was still throbbing.

"Your hand." Teresa scrambled to her feet with the help of one of the security guys who was watching Josh closely. "I completely forgot. Come on, we'll get you that ice."

Teresa walked to the back of the room and asked

the bartender to put some ice in an ice bucket for her. The man obliged.

They sat at a table at the back of the room, which was now empty, aside from the security team members and a bomb-sniffing dog they'd brought in.

She carefully set the vintage glass art deco style ice bucket on the table, shifted the ice around, then put his hand inside it.

He winced momentarily. "So about your brother… why do you think he showed up here severely impaired after dropping off the map?" Liam asked the question gingerly. "And since you two haven't talked, how did he know where you were?"

She was grateful for the kindness in Liam's tone. After her conversation with Matt, it was the lifeline she needed.

"Those are excellent questions, Liam. I only wish I had answers. And in Joshua's current condition, I don't expect we'll get coherent answers anytime soon."

"Does he drink a lot?"

"He did for a time in college, when he fell in with the wrong crowd. But what he's been up to of late, I'm ashamed to say I don't know." She shifted her gaze to where Joshua still lay on the stage. "I've been too consumed with my own issues. Trying to keep my business afloat and my name off the front page of the paper."

Teresa sighed, her hand resting on his wrist. "I haven't been a very good sister, have I?"

"Don't blame yourself for this. Josh is a grown

man, capable of making his own choices. You can't babysit him for the rest of his life."

"Maybe." Teresa sounded unconvinced. "In the meantime, I need to find transportation home for us."

"You and Josh can ride back to Seattle on my plane." Liam clamped a gentle hand on her arm before she could get up from the table.

"That's sweet of you, Liam. But what happened tonight makes it abundantly clear that I need to stay away from you. If I don't, I'll end up bringing Christopher Corporation down, too."

"Teresa—"

"I have to go before Matt changes his mind about pressing charges. He might even consider suing me. I wasn't to blame for the mudslide, but the same can't be said tonight."

"Don't worry about Matt. He's angry now, but he'll get over it."

"Like your mother has?" she asked, then shook her head. "I'm sorry. I shouldn't have said that."

"No, you shouldn't have. Given what my mother still believes about you, you can understand why she's holding a grudge." Liam hated what his mother had done and that she wasn't willing to reconsider her position. But he understood her resentment. In fact, he'd shared her righteous anger just a few weeks ago.

"That's all the more reason I need to stay away from you and from your company. I couldn't forgive myself if something happened to you or to your father's legacy because of his generosity to me." She stood.

"I can help you, Teresa. You said it yourself, I'm a fixer, of sorts. If we work together, I know we can—"

"Josh is my brother, and this is my problem, Liam. I won't bring you into this any more than I already have." Her chest ached at the thought of not being able to keep their planned date later that evening. "This is something Joshua and I need to figure out."

"So what are you going to do? You don't honestly expect to get a commercial flight back to Seattle tonight, do you?" Liam removed his hand from the bucket and dried it on a towel.

"Looking for a ride back to Seattle tonight?" Brooks Abbingdon approached their table and picked up his cell phone, which he'd apparently left behind when he was forced to exit the ballroom. "Since the festivities ended earlier than expected, I'm flying back tonight. Leaving in a little over an hour if you'd like to come along."

Liam tensed. If even half of the rumors about what a playboy Brooks Abbingdon was were true, he didn't want Teresa flying back to Seattle on the man's private jet.

"It isn't just me. My brother would be coming, too." Teresa pointed to Joshua, who was just starting to stir as the men stood watch over him.

"That's your brother?" Brooks gave a long, low whistle. "Is he gonna be a problem?"

"No, he won't. I promise," Teresa said. "But if

you don't feel comfortable having him on the plane, I can understand that."

"As long as you can keep him on a short leash, I'm fine with it. Truth is, we all have family like that, now don't we?" Brooks winked. "My car will be downstairs in a little over a half an hour. I'll see you then." He nodded at Liam and then walked away.

"Teresa, you don't need to go with him. You can go with me tomorrow morning. You can both stay in my cottage tonight, if you need to."

"No," she whispered, her eyes filled with tears. "I won't get you any more mixed up in this. But thank you for offering and for being a listening ear."

She leaned down to kiss his cheek, but he turned and pressed his lips to hers instead. A kiss that sent electricity down her spine and filled her body with heat as she remembered what had happened between them earlier. And that it would never happen again.

She slipped out of Liam's embrace and walked to the stage to collect her brother before Matt Richmond returned.

The security guy agreed to help her brother to the concierge's office, right by the hotel entrance, where they would wait out of sight for Brooks's car service to arrive. And he promised to stay with him until she and Josh left the property. It was less of a favor to her and more of an order from Matt Richmond, she was sure. But she appreciated it just the same.

She would need to coordinate with her remaining staff, go back to her room and pack all of her things and meet Brooks at the front door of the hotel in twenty minutes flat.

"Melva, I'll be checking out tonight." Teresa approached the front desk in a hurry. She apologized to the beautiful woman standing at the desk for interrupting.

"I'm so sorry, Teresa." Melva frowned. "Under the circumstances, I hate to ask, but this woman is—"

"You're Jessie Humphrey's sister. Jennifer?" Teresa had seen photos of the two women together on Jessie's Instagram account.

"Geneva." The woman smiled warmly as she slipped her hand in Teresa's. "It's a pleasure to meet you. I flew all the way in from Amsterdam to surprise my little sister, but both of my flights were delayed. It seems I missed both of her performances."

"You did, I'm sorry. They were both brilliant." Teresa nodded impatiently. She had no doubt Brooks would pull off with or without her. "What can I do for you, Geneva?"

"I wanted to surprise my sister, but she isn't in her room and she isn't answering her phone. Do you know where I can find her?"

"I don't." Teresa thought better of telling the woman that she'd last seen her sister leaving the ballroom with her ex, Gideon Johns.

"And I can't allow her to enter Ms. Humphrey's room without her express permission," Melva piped. "I'm not really sure what to do with her until her sister pops up."

"Right. Of course. And the hotel is completely

booked." Teresa thought for a minute. "I'll tell you what…my room is paid for through Monday. You'll just need to leave a card on file for incidentals and we can switch the room over to Mrs.…."

"*Ms.* Humphrey." A pained look dimmed the light in the woman's eyes momentarily before her easy smile slid back into place. "That would be wonderful. Thank you, Teresa."

"Give her my room number and a key," Teresa instructed Melva. "Just give me thirty minutes and I'll be gone. Perhaps you'll even run into Jessie in the bar while you wait."

Teresa said her goodbyes to both women and hurried to her room to pack as quickly as she could.

Twenty-One

Jessie collected her makeup and changed out of her Laylahni Couture ball gown in the greenroom while Gideon waited.

Her head was still spinning with all of the chaos that had ensued once the man made his way onto the stage.

She was in the midst of saying her thank-yous and had one encore song left to perform. Why couldn't the drunk party crasher have waited until then to jump onstage?

Jessie stared in the mirror. Her eyes were puffy and red from the tears that wouldn't seem to stop flowing once they'd started. She'd held them back until she'd entered the bathroom alone. But Gideon would know she'd been crying the moment he saw her eyes. Unless…

She dug into her leather Gregory Sylvia hobo bag and pulled out her black Bôhten shades and slid them on. She hated doing the obnoxious sunglasses-at-night celebrity thing, but right now it was more important to protect her pride.

Jessie put a satin-lined slouch hat on her head and tucked her curls beneath it. Then she emerged from the bathroom wearing a pair of GRLFRND high-waist, ripped skinny jeans, a T-shirt and kitten heels. She carried the beautiful Laylahni Couture gown over one arm in a garment bag.

"You came out just in the nick of time." Gideon smiled softly, taking all of her bags except her purse from her. "I was just about to come in after you to make sure you were okay."

"If that's a pun because of the song I sang to-night…it's too soon."

Jessie exited through the exterior door rather than going through the lobby of the hotel. Party guests still milled around and Nicolette Ryan and her cameraman were camped out there.

Nicolette had texted her and asked her for an exclusive interview about the incident as she and Gideon made their escape to the greenroom.

She declined.

Nicolette seemed understanding and sympathetic. But Jessie had no desire to relive her performance going up in flames. All because some guy who couldn't hold his liquor decided to be a complete ass during the biggest moment of her career.

"I wasn't trying to be cute," Gideon said. "What

happened was no laughing matter. The guy turned out to be harmless this time. But what if he hadn't been?" Gideon seemed especially perturbed at the possibility that something could've happened to her. "And I know how important that performance was to you. But, Jessie, you nailed it. Your set last night was terrific. But what you did tonight…it was brilliant. You should be damned proud of yourself."

"Thanks." She came to a halt at the fork in the path and turned to face him. "And thank you for not being an ass about me writing these songs about you."

Gideon gave her a half grin. "Not everyone can say that they inspired someone to write a song. Let alone several. Especially one as good as 'Okay.'"

"Did you really like the song or are you just being unbelievably gracious about the whole thing?" She practically held her breath waiting for his response.

"Of course I really loved the song. Every damn person in that room loved it. Everything about it was perfect. The lyrics. The music. The way you sang the song…you poured your heart out on that stage."

"Until random drunk guy came and stomped on it." She took a deep breath and reminded herself there was no crying in record deals. This was a tough business. If she was going to break down in tears every time things didn't go her way, she needed to find another dream to chase.

"I know you're bummed about what happened, but let me tell you something, Jessie. Anyone who saw that performance tonight, anyone who experienced it as deeply as I did…they will never, ever forget it. I can assure you of that."

"Thanks." Jessie's mouth quirked involuntarily in the slightest twinge of a smile. Her cheeks heated, and her body tingled with electricity from his nearness.

"So, am I walking you back to your room?" Gideon asked.

Neither of them had moved beyond the fork in the path. Either they could take the route back to the hotel where her room was located or they could take the path that led to his cottage.

"Actually, if the invitation still stands, I could really use that nightcap you offered." Her heart raced as she anticipated his response.

He studied her for a moment, as if he was debating the wisdom of taking her back to his cottage. "Of course it still stands."

They turned up the path toward the private cottages.

"Chase and Dixon seemed blown away by your performance," he noted. "I wouldn't be surprised if both of them contact your agent, eager to work with you. You knocked them off their feet."

"They seemed really into it when I was performing. Dixon was right there with me the whole time. He even started a standing ovation."

"That was pretty incredible."

"It was." She couldn't help smiling. "Chase didn't really seem to get on board until I performed 'Okay.' But their table was among the first to be ushered out of the room." The disappointment of not securing a meeting with either Chase or Dixon weighed on her.

Then there was the matter of Gideon.

She glanced over at him. He was handsome and tall with broad shoulders and such an incredible smile. He was still the smart, funny, determined guy she'd known back then. But he was also a successful businessman who employed members of his community and gave generously to important causes.

She'd always admired Gideon and expected great things of him, regardless of what her father and sister believed. But he'd exceeded her wildest expectations.

And she wanted to be with him more than ever. Not because of the schoolgirl crush she'd once harbored for him. But because he was exactly the kind of man she wanted in her life.

If she told Gideon that, he'd think she was still a silly, immature girl with a crush. After all, how could she know in just a few days that she wanted to be with him?

She just did.

That day when she'd shown up at Gideon's door, she told him that he was the only person who really understood her. That he got her in a way her parents, sister and even friends didn't. She was sure that Gideon was her soul mate. And it was her that he was meant to be with.

He'd probably thought she was a melodramatic teenager who didn't know what she was talking about. But here they were fifteen years later and the more she got reacquainted with Gideon, the more she believed she'd been right all along.

All of her fears about her career aside, what if they really were meant to be together? Shouldn't she at least be brave enough to give it a try?

"You're awfully quiet, Jess." Gideon set her bags down on the doorstep of his cottage, but he didn't open the door. "If you'd rather I walk you back to your room, I understand. You've had an exhausting day. You're probably ready to call it a night after everything that's—"

Jessie drew in a deep breath, clutched Gideon's tuxedo shirt and lifted onto her toes, pressing her mouth to his in a tentative kiss that built slowly. Gideon slipped his arms around her waist and hauled her body against his, the intensity of their kiss building.

Finally, she forced herself to pull away, her eyes fluttering open as they met his. "Does that answer your question?"

Gideon poured a glass of sauvignon blanc and handed it to Jessie.

She took a sip and made a purring sound that sent a shiver up his spine and made him want to cut the formalities and tell her exactly what he'd been feeling these past few days.

That he hadn't stopped thinking about her since she'd walked through the doors of that hotel. That he wanted her in his bed.

There was something so compelling about Jessie.

Compelling enough that the idea of missing out on it was stronger than the fear of what he'd be letting go.

"You're right, this wine is fantastic." Her words jarred him from his thoughts.

Gideon filled her wineglass and then poured himself two fingers of whiskey. He sipped his whiskey slowly, then sank onto the opposite sofa.

He crossed one ankle over his knee and assessed the woman seated across from him as she sipped her wine.

"A lot has happened tonight. I know you're disappointed, but maybe it wasn't as bad as you think. We should look at the live stream from the event."

"No. Please." Her bravado faded momentarily. "I shut my phone off for the rest of the night. I don't want to see it. Not yet. Just let me live in my little fantasy realm where I killed it on stage tonight and everything is right with the world."

"It isn't a fantasy, Jess. You *did* kill it on stage tonight. And I'll bet that ninety-nine percent of the people who saw your performance would agree."

"And that one percent?" Jessie raised a brow.

"They have terrible taste in music, so they don't count." He grinned when she laughed. He'd always loved the joyous sound of her laugh. "Seriously, if the vast majority of listeners think you were amazing, why do you care about what an infinitesimal fraction of people think?"

"It's the nature of the creative beast. I can't help it." Jessie shrugged. "Besides, I learn more from my critical reviews than I do from the glowing ones that tell me exactly what I want to hear." She paced the floor. "Which is why I need to work with producers like Chase and Dixon. They have this uncanny ability to take a track that might seem good on the surface and turn it into something spectacular."

"About that..." Gideon set his glass down. "I know you asked me not to interfere on this, but what if I could pull some strings and get you a meeting with one or both of them?"

Jessie folded her arms and plopped down in her seat. "I want a meeting with them, of course. But I'd like to do this on my own. The same way you built your business on your own. You didn't rely on anyone else."

"Not true." He leaned forward. "I owe my success to a lot of men and women who were willing to give me opportunities and teach me what they'd learned." Gideon shrugged. "I pay their generosity and kindness forward by doing the same."

Jessie had kicked off her heels and padded over to the sideboard where the bottle of wine was chilling. She refilled her glass of wine, then sat on the sofa with her feet folded beneath her. "I've read business articles about you. They always call you a self-made billionaire." Jessie didn't seem convinced.

"Because it's the more compelling story." Gideon groaned. He gave credit to the people who had helped him every single chance he got. But the importance of those relationships was inevitably minimized in magazines and interviews.

"My assistant Landon…the guy is a work in progress, for sure." Gideon chuckled, thinking of some of their conversations. "But he's good at what he does, and he has a hell of a lot of potential. If I can help him get closer to his goals, even if that means leaving my company and striking out on his own, I'm going to support him any way I can. So let me do the same for you."

Jessie drank a gulp of her wine, her eyes not meeting his. "I don't like the idea of owing anyone anything. It gives people too much power over you."

"You think I'd want something in return?" He had to admit that one hurt. He thought she knew him better than that. Yes, it was fifteen years ago, but did she really think he'd changed that much? "Why would you ever think that?"

"It's happened before with someone I trusted."

Now he understood, and he wished he could give the fucker who'd made her feel that way a savage beatdown just to show him how it felt to be vulnerable.

"What happened?" Gideon sat on the edge of his seat, both of his feet firmly planted on the floor. "And whose ass do I need to beat?" There was a ticking in a vein in his forehead.

"Gideon, no." Jessie moved over to sit beside him. Her warmth enveloped him and her faint floral scent calmed the anger bubbling inside him over her revelation about her mentor. "I don't want to talk about that or the shitshow my performance turned into. Tonight, I want to talk about us."

She'd said it. Finally gotten it out into the open where they could discuss it like two rational adults. Though he found it difficult to have a reasonable discussion when she was sitting this close.

Jessie had already shed the sunglasses. Now she slipped off the hat and tossed it onto the sofa beside her, refluffing her headful of dark curls. Her short manicured nails were painted a deeper shade of pink and every other nail was affixed with a design.

"I'd like that." Gideon turned toward her and loosened his tie. "Spending these past few days with you has been special for me. I never stopped caring for you, Jess. The feelings I had for you then weren't romantic, but you were incredibly important to me. The loss of our friendship hurt as much as being dumped by Geneva."

Jessie frowned. Was it because he'd mentioned Geneva or because he'd admitted his feelings for her back then were platonic?

"One of my biggest regrets was how badly I'd bungled things between us. That my insensitivity that day hurt you." He traced the back of her hand with his thumb.

Jessie didn't respond to his confession, but her sensual lips spread in a slow smile. She leaned in, raised a hand to his cheek and kissed him again.

He wrapped his arms around her, his hand pressed to her back. Loving the feel of her in his arms and the taste of her warm mouth as he slid his tongue between her lips. He lost himself in her kiss. Lost all sense of time and place. Set aside his fears about what this meant for them.

He only knew he wanted more of this. More of her.

The longer he kissed her, the more sure he was that he would never get enough of her quiet murmurs. Or the way her soft, curvy body fit so neatly against the hard planes of his. That he would never tire of holding her in his arms.

Suddenly, Jessie pressed against his chest, creating space between them. She dragged her gaze to his, her chest heaving as she caught her breath. "There's one thing I need to know. It's about Geneva."

He already knew what she was going to ask, but she needed to say the words. "What do you want to know?"

She tucked strands of her hair behind one ear. "I need to know…if there was a chance for the two of you again, would you want it?"

"No." He kissed one corner of her mouth and then the other. "I loved your sister, but that was a long, long time ago. And we were never right for each other." He left a slow, lingering kiss on her mouth. Then pressed his lips to her ear. "It isn't Geneva I want, Jess. Or haven't you noticed?"

He lay her back on the sofa, his length pressed to her belly as he kissed her until they were both breathless.

He dropped kisses on her forehead and her eyelids. "Do you believe me?"

She nodded, her gaze meeting his. "I do," she whispered.

"Good." He kissed her again, savoring the taste of her sweet mouth and the feel of her body beneath his. "Because from the moment you strutted into that hotel lobby, I've only wanted you."

Twenty-Two

Teresa sat in the tan buttery leather seat on Brooks Abbingdon's private plane and fastened her seat belt. Then she double-checked to make sure her brother's seat belt was secure, since he was still fairly out of it.

One thing Teresa knew for sure, Joshua wasn't drunk. His clothing and skin were completely devoid of the scent of alcohol. Still, there was clearly something wrong with him.

Joshua had roused enough to walk onto the plane, but he was still babbling incoherently about rich liars and losers and the truth being exposed. When he wasn't ranting, he would doze off. So getting the truth from Joshua wasn't an option. In fact, as out of it as he seemed, she wondered if Josh would remember any of this, even once he became lucid.

He mumbled something that sounded vaguely like *sorry, love you, sis*. But then again, maybe that was just what Teresa wanted to hear. Something to make her feel the slightest bit better about the fact that her career was over. In fact, she was shocked that Brooks wanted anything to do with her once he learned that the party disrupter was her brother.

Joshua leaned his head on her shoulder, his dark brown hair tickling her nose. He muttered something again. This time she clearly heard *sorry* and *screwed up again*. Those words were followed by more incoherent babbling.

Joshua rubbed at his arm, complaining that it hurt like a bitch. *That* she heard quite clearly. He kept rubbing at his left arm, so she rolled up his sleeve and looked at it.

Teresa turned her head to one side and then the other, zeroing in on a small, nearly invisible mark on his forearm. She rummaged in her bag and took out her lighted pocket magnifier. Now she could see clearly what it was that Josh kept scratching at. It was a tiny, isolated puncture wound.

She breathed a sigh of relief that there was just the single mark. She checked his other arm and his ankle and saw no additional marks. If Joshua was an addict, he'd have several puncture wounds on his body, not just one. Which suggested that this was an isolated incident. But the more important question was, had her brother willingly injected himself with something?

"Your brother doesn't look very good." Brooks

switched to the seat across from her once they were able to freely move about the plane.

"He's been conscious more often, and I'm beginning to understand more of what he's saying." Teresa swept the hair from her brother's sweaty forehead.

"Should I request that the driver take him to a hospital once we land?" Brooks studied Josh with concern.

She could only imagine how inconvenient it would be to have someone die on one's private plane. Teresa banished the snarky comment from her head. After all, Brooks had offered to help when she was persona non grata to everyone but Liam.

"No, but thank you for the offer just the same." Teresa smiled warmly at Brooks.

"You're sure?" He didn't seem convinced that it was a good idea.

In any other circumstance, Teresa would've insisted that they rush Joshua to the hospital. There they could identify the substance he'd been given and flush it from his system.

But that could mean trouble for Joshua. She'd paid a hefty price to ensure that his earlier offenses hadn't ended up on his record. If she took him to the hospital, the staff would need to report the incident. Was this all Josh's doing or was someone willing to put Josh's life in danger to ruin hers?

Nicolette's warning to Liam that they should be careful whom they trusted suddenly came to mind.

"I'm sure. Thank you, Brooks."

Teresa heaved a small sigh of relief when Brooks

nodded and walked back to his seat. She glanced down at her still-shaking hands as she deliberated her next move.

Liam paced the floor of his cottage, still trying to figure out how everything had gone off the rails so quickly. The weekend started with so much promise and ended in a disaster, for which it would most likely be remembered. Particularly since the entire circus had been captured live on streaming video.

He was furious with Joshua for ruining his best friend's event and decimating what remained of the reputation of and goodwill toward Teresa and Limitless Events. He honestly couldn't imagine that her business could recover from what had just happened, especially in light of the fact that the person who'd crashed the party had been her brother.

Add to that his rant about rich people being liars and losers…well, the wealthy set could overlook a lot of things. Calling them out like that wasn't one of them.

Liam's phone rang. He dug it out of his inside jacket pocket, hoping it was Teresa saying she'd changed her mind and would accept his offered plane ride tomorrow.

Shit.

He heaved a long sigh and answered the telephone. "Hello, Mother. What can I do for you?"

"You can stop making a fool of yourself by your insistence on associating with that Teresa person," Catherine Christopher said without hesitation. "You know what she's done, who she was to your father, and how she destroyed our family. Emilia Cartwright one of my oldest and closest friends, sent me a video of you dancing with that woman as if neither of you had a care in the world. And, just as I predicted, the evening turned into a disaster. That woman destroys everything in her path. And that poor singer, assaulted! Just horrible!"

"You watched the live stream?" That didn't sound like something that would interest his mother at all. If she wasn't in the room holding court as the center of attention, she simply wasn't interested.

"Only because I received dozens of calls from people who saw you canoodling with that witch earlier and I wanted to see what else was going on."

"We were dancing together on a crowded dance floor. It's not as if I had her up against the wall in the back of the room."

"Don't be vulgar, Liam." His mother's voice was strained. "I did everything I possibly could to warn your friend Matt Richmond not to associate his brand with that woman, but he just wouldn't listen. Now that millions of people have seen the train wreck his party turned into, he's the laughingstock of the entire internet. And who would want to attend another of his parties? A life-threatening disaster is practically sure to ensue."

"You're being melodramatic, Mother. You weren't there, and it wasn't seen by millions. The situation wasn't that serious. Matt's security team just wanted to be extra cautious after the man was able to get onto the stage. It was an overreaction to their initial screwup."

"Where is that woman now?"

Liam hesitated before responding. "Gone. Matt asked her to leave."

"Good riddance. All of us will be better off with Teresa St. Claire out of the picture."

Liam ended the call with his mother and gulped his Manhattan. Maybe his mother's life would be better without Teresa St. Claire in the mix. But he'd felt a gnawing in his chest from the moment she'd walked out the door.

Twenty-Three

Jessie was in heaven. Gideon's kiss, his touch, had been every bit as wonderful as her mind had imagined. But as the intensity of their kiss escalated, she wanted more.

Gideon had rolled them over so Jessie lay on top of him. She shifted so that she straddled him on the sofa. Both of them murmured at the sensation when she placed her hands on his chest and rocked the apex of her thighs against his steely length. He cupped her bottom, bringing her closer as she ground her hips against him, the sensation between them building.

He still seemed tentative. Or maybe he wanted to let her set the pace. But she knew what she wanted. She wanted his large, strong hands to caress her bare skin. To glide her hands over his. And she wanted him inside her.

Jessie grasped the hem of her shirt and lifted it over her head, tossing it aside. Gideon quickly removed her sheer black bra and dropped it to the floor, too.

He pulled her toward him and laved one of her tight, beaded nipples. Jessie arched into him with an involuntary whimper as he licked and sucked the sensitive tip.

Gideon gently scraped his teeth over the tight bud and she cursed under her breath at the sensation his actions elicited in the warm space between her thighs. He shifted his focus to her other breast, lavishing it with the same attention.

"God, I want you, Jess," he whispered against her skin.

His beard scraped her flesh, adding to the mélange of sensations.

Gideon's gaze met hers as he unbuttoned her jeans, then slowly unzipped them.

Jessie sank her teeth into her lower lip and lifted her hips, eager to help him slide the garment off one leg and then the other. He stood suddenly, taking her by surprise as he lifted her. She wrapped her long legs around him and held on to his neck as he carried her to the bed and laid her beneath the covers.

She had wanted this for as long as she could remember. But now that she was here in Gideon's bed, her hands trembled and butterflies flitted in her belly.

Her anticipation grew as Gideon slowly removed his tie and then his jacket. As if he was putting on a show just for her. He took off his shirt to reveal his strong, muscular chest and chiseled abs. Then he slowly unzipped his tuxedo pants and allowed the fabric to pool around his ankles.

Dayum.

Jessie swallowed hard, her eyes tracing the pronounced outline of his thick erection beneath his charcoal-gray boxers. She couldn't tear her gaze away from the darkened circle over the tip.

She licked her lower lip, the space between her thighs throbbing as she was struck by the sudden desire to taste him there.

Gideon reached into the bedside drawer and removed one of the foil packets stocked by the hotel. He slipped out of his boxers and sheathed himself, crawling into bed with her.

She'd never seen anything sexier than this man, completely naked, crawling toward her. Like a panther in pursuit of his next conquest.

He dragged her sheer panties down her legs and settled between her thighs as he kissed her again, his tongue searching hers.

Jessie wrapped her legs around his waist and her arms around his back as he kissed her. His hips rocked against hers.

His kiss was hungry and demanding. Making her more desperate for him. The space between her thighs pulsed and her nipples prickled as they moved against the hair on his broad chest.

Gideon broke their kiss, leaving her breathless and wanting. He trailed kisses down her neck and shoulder as he shifted off of her. She immediately missed the weight and warmth of his strong, hard body.

He moved beside her and thrust his hand between her thighs, gliding his fingers through her wetness, over her sensitive nub. She whimpered, overwhelmed by the sensation as she writhed against his hand. He inserted two large fingers, then three. Sliding them in and out of her as his thumb teased her hardened clit.

Gideon brought her close to the edge, her legs shaking. Then he'd back off just enough to keep her from going over.

"Gideon, please." It wasn't like her to whimper or beg. But she was so close, her body trembling with need. "I want you."

"And I have never wanted anyone as much as I want you, Jess." He pulled his fingers from inside her, moving them over the needy bundle of nerves and all of the slick, sensitive flesh surrounding it.

The muscles of her belly tensed and she cried out his name, the dam inside her bursting. Overflowing with intense pleasure.

He kissed her neck and shoulders as her body shuddered. Finally, he pressed the head of his erection to her entrance, slowly pushing his width inside her.

Jessie dug her short fingernails into his back, her body tense as Gideon slowly entered her.

"Relax, Jess," he whispered. "Breathe. I would never hurt you."

Jessie hadn't realized that she was holding her breath and her muscles were clenched in anticipation. She breathed in and out slowly, her eyes pressed shut.

Gideon rewarded her with a slow, sweet, tender kiss.

"Open your eyes, Jess." His voice was low and deep. "I want to see those beautiful brown eyes while I'm inside you. And I want you to see exactly what you do to me. How badly I want you."

He moved inside her slowly, allowing her body to adjust to the sensation of being completely filled by him.

They moved together, their skin slick with sweat. Her belly tensed as her heels dug into the mattress. Another orgasm rocked her to her core. She called his name, her body quivering.

Gideon tensed, her name on his lips as he tumbled over the edge into pleasure. The pulsing of his cock pulled her in deeper, her walls contracting around him.

Jessie released a contented sigh, her head lolling back on the pillow. She smiled up at Gideon. His forehead was beaded with sweat and his chest still heaved. He traced her cheekbone with his thumb.

"That was amazing." He kissed her. "Is it bad that I already want you again?"

"No. Because I plan on taking every meal right here in this bed until Monday morning when I have to go back to…" Her words trailed as the reality of the situation dimmed the buzz she was feeling.

"Let's not think about Monday morning right now." He caressed her cheek.

"Good plan."

Gideon dropped a tender kiss on her lips, then lay on his back and gathered her in his arms, pulling the covers around them.

Jessie pressed her cheek to his chest, their intense encounter replaying in her head. She tried to do as Gideon asked and not think about Monday. But she couldn't escape the knowledge that in thirty-six hours they would go their separate ways.

Gideon cradled Jessie in his arms as she slept soundly with her hand and cheek pressed to his chest. Her quiet exhalations skittered across his skin.

He couldn't remember the last time he'd felt so content. Or the last time he'd been with someone who made him feel the things that Jessie did. He glided a hand up and down the smooth skin of her bare arm as she slept.

It was well after one in the morning, but it had been several hours since he'd last checked his email. Gideon reached for his phone on the nightstand and turned it back on.

He checked his email, directing the light from the phone away from Jessie so he wouldn't disturb her sleep. He replied to a few urgent messages, then noticed that he had several alerts for Jessie's name.

She hadn't wanted to see the video, and he got that. But at least one of them should see it. That way he could prepare her if it was as bad as she believed.

When he followed the link to view the video, there were already thousands of remarks. He sucked in a deep breath and started to read through them. He was pleasantly surprised.

"Jessie." He couldn't help waking her. She'd been so disappointed about how the performance ended. She needed to see this. "Sweetheart, you've got to see what people are saying about your performance last night."

She grumbled and buried her face in his chest before finally rolling over on her back and propping herself up on her elbows.

"All right, all right," she mumbled. "Let's get this over with."

He played the video and scrolled through some of the comments. The more she read them, the more excited she got.

"Oh my God. Did you see this? Dixon Benedict left an amazing comment. He said I'm one of the most talented singer/songwriters he's ever seen. He even says he'd love to work with me someday." Jessie sat up in bed, her back pressed against the headboard as she scrolled through the comments, most of which were rave reviews of her performance.

"This is incredible. Thank you, Gideon." She handed him back his phone and kissed him. "And I really do appreciate your offer to broker a meeting between me and Chase or Dixon. But I'd like to give it one more try on my own first. If I need your help, I'll ask. I promise."

"Whatever you want, beautiful." He cradled her

cheek. "I told you, you're a star, Jessie Humphrey. And you're going to do amazing things." He kissed her.

She gave him a sly smile as she reached into the drawer of the bedside table and climbed atop him. "There are a few amazing things I'd like to do right now."

"Oh yeah?" He rolled them over so that he hovered over her. "I'm all for that." He leaned down and kissed her. Then he made love to her again.

Jessie returned to her room on Sunday afternoon to gather some of her toiletries and fresh clothing. Gideon sat on the sofa watching the stock market news as he made calls to his assistant Landon.

There was a knock at her hotel room door.

"Gideon, would you get that, please?" Jessie called from the bathroom as she packed up her makeup and facial cleanser.

"Sure thing," he replied.

She'd expected him to call to her that it was the hotel staff or maybe Teresa or Matt looking for her. But there was silence in the other room.

"Gideon, who is it?" Jessie walked out into the main living space of the suite. She was stunned to see a face that resembled her own.

"Geneva, what are you doing here?" Jessie stammered. "I thought you were still in Amsterdam." Her voice faded and she wrapped her arms around herself.

"I was, but I thought I'd surprise my little sis. You said I should come to visit, so I thought I'd pop into Napa first and catch your performances. But my flights were delayed and I got in after your set ended last night." Geneva took a few steps closer to her sister. "But I saw the videos. Jessie, you were incredible. How is it that I didn't realize just how talented my sister is?"

Geneva opened her arms and Jessie stepped into them, hugging her sister tightly. Neither her parents nor Geneva had supported her decision to go into music. So it felt good to hear her sister's validation. It wasn't something she needed, but she hadn't realized until now how much she'd wanted it.

Her sister cupped her cheek and smiled, then turned to Gideon. She gave him what Jessie knew to be a forced smile.

"Gideon, it's good to see you." Geneva nodded toward him, awkwardness lingering between them.

"You, too, Geneva." He shoved his hands in his pockets, not moving toward her.

"So…you two, huh?" Geneva glanced from Jessie to Gideon, then back when neither of them responded. "Since when?"

"Since this weekend." Gideon pulled one hand out of his pocket and threaded his fingers through Jessie's. He squeezed her hand. "We hadn't seen each other in a really long time. We got a chance to get reacquainted during the retreat."

Jessie breathed a sigh of relief. She hadn't told Geneva or anyone else about the day she'd gone to Gideon's apartment. Maybe she'd tell her sister someday. But there was already enough tension between them. She wouldn't add to it.

Gideon wrapped an arm around Jessie's waist, as if he knew she needed his reassurance that he had no regrets about choosing her.

"I know you missed Jessie's show, Geneva, but there's lots to do here in Napa. Why don't I take you ladies to lunch later?"

"Great idea, Gideon." Jessie smiled at him gratefully. She turned to her sister. "What do you say, Gen? The food here is amazing and so is the wine."

"I'd like that." Geneva put on her biggest smile as she wiped dampness from beneath her eyes. "Can I meet you at the restaurant in say…an hour?"

"Geneva, I'm sorry if me being with Gideon feels uncomfortable right now. You're my sister and I love you. I'd never intentionally hurt you." Jessie took both of Geneva's hands in hers. "But… I love him. I think I always have." She glanced over her shoulder at Gideon. He grinned and mouthed the words, *I love you, too.* Jessie turned back to her sister. "And I did see him first."

"Yes, you did, Squirt." Geneva called Jessie by her childhood nickname through a teary-eyed laugh. "I guess technically I stole him first."

"You totally did." Jessie laughed, her eyes damp, too.

"Oh, Jessie." Geneva cradled her cheek. Her sister's smile seemed genuine, despite the tears that spilled down her face. "I'm so happy for you. For both of you." She turned to Gideon. "I've only ever wanted the best for both of you. I'm glad that the two sweetest people I've ever known eventually found happiness together. Things are just as they should be."

Geneva hugged Jessie again. Then she hugged Gideon. "You've always been a great guy, Gideon. So whatever happens between you two, I know you'll be good to my little sister." She turned to leave. "I'll see you two downstairs in an hour."

Jessie sighed with relief when the door closed behind Geneva. She turned to Gideon. "I'm sorry to have said that here, like this. I know it's only been a weekend and I wouldn't possibly expect you to—"

"Jess, breathe." Gideon pulled her to him. "Spending time with you this weekend reminded me what a rare gift it is to have someone in my life who believed in me from the beginning, when I had nothing. You were always in my corner, Jess. I want that again, and I want to do the same for you."

He pressed a soft kiss to her lips and stroked her cheek. "And when I said I love you, too, I meant it. I wanted to say it earlier, but I was afraid I'd scare you off."

"Your heart is racing." Jessie could feel Gideon's heart thumping against her palm, pressed to his chest. "Are you sure you're not the one who's terrified by this?"

"I haven't opened myself up to anyone like this in a really long time. So yeah…it feels a little scary. But I have never been so sure about what I want. And what I want is you."

"This weekend has been so amazing. What happens when we try to translate it into an actual relationship?" Jessie frowned, her eyes searching his. "I'm in New York and you're in Seattle. You'll be traveling to the Middle East and, eventually, I'll be out on tour."

"I know it seems insurmountable, but we don't get many do-overs in life. So I don't intend to take this second chance for granted."

"You know how long I've wanted this, Gideon. But I've worked really hard for my career, too. I don't want to give that up, either."

"I'd never ask you to." He kissed her forehead. "Look, no one said this would be easy, but for you, I'm willing to make sacrifices. I'd always planned to open an office in New York. Looks like I'll be opening it sooner than I thought." He kissed her again as he hauled her against him. "And I already own a penthouse in Manhattan with the perfect space to install a recording studio."

"You'd move to New York for me?" Jess pulled back to gaze up at him. "Are you serious?"

"I really do love you, Jessie Humphrey." He smiled. "And I look forward to making a life together. I don't know what the future holds, but I promise you, as long as you're all in, I am, too."

Jessie's eyes stung with tears and her heart felt full. She honestly couldn't ever remember being happier than she was right now. Lifting onto her toes, she kissed the man she'd loved for as long as she could remember.

Epilogue

An insidious grin spanned Catherine Christopher's face as she counted out a stack of crisp one-hundred-dollar bills. Liam's mother handed the stack to the man standing beside her desk.

"That went even better than expected." The woman snickered. "Everyone believes that Joshua St. Claire was out of his mind drunk or worse, high on something vile. What did you give him, anyway?"

The man opened his mouth to speak, but Catherine held up a hand and turned her head.

"On second thought, it's better if I don't know. The only thing that matters is that the little bitch got exactly what she deserves," Catherine announced gleefully.

"St. Claire probably won't even remember that he

was drugged." The man counted the bills for himself before shoving them into his pocket.

"Perfect." Catherine smiled as she looked out the window and surveyed her vast estate. "His sister won't see what's coming, either. Just wait until Teresa St. Claire finds out what I have planned for her next."

* * * * *

What does Catherine have planned?
Will Liam and Teresa ever find their happy ending?

Don't miss a single episode in the Dynasties:
Secrets of the A-List quartet!

Book One
Tempted by Scandal *by Karen Booth*

Book Two
Taken by Storm *by Cat Schield*

Book Three
Seduced by Second Chances *by Reese Ryan*

Book Four
Redeemed by Passion *by Joss Wood*

Available August 2019

Get 4 FREE REWARDS!

We'll send you 2 FREE Books <u>plus</u> 2 FREE Mystery Gifts.

Harlequin® Desire books feature heroes who have it all: wealth, status, incredible good looks... everything but the right woman.

FREE Value Over **$20**

YES! Please send me 2 FREE Harlequin® Desire novels and my 2 FREE gifts (gifts are worth about $10 retail). After receiving them, if I don't wish to receive any more books, I can return the shipping statement marked "cancel." If I don't cancel, I will receive 6 brand-new novels every month and be billed just $4.55 per book in the U.S. or $5.24 per book in Canada. That's a savings of at least 13% off the cover price! It's quite a bargain! Shipping and handling is just 50¢ per book in the U.S. and $1.25 per book in Canada.* I understand that accepting the 2 free books and gifts places me under no obligation to buy anything. I can always return a shipment and cancel at any time. The free books and gifts are mine to keep no matter what I decide.

225/326 HDN GNND

Name (please print)

Address   Apt. #

City   State/Province   Zip/Postal Code

Mail to the Reader Service:
IN U.S.A.: P.O. Box 1341, Buffalo, NY 14240-8531
IN CANADA: P.O. Box 603, Fort Erie, Ontario L2A 5X3

Want to try 2 free books from another series! Call 1-800-873-8635 or visit www.ReaderService.com.

HD19R3

"You sure like coming up to me guns blazing, Jamie Dodge.
Just saying whatever it is that's on your mind. No concern for
the fallout of it. Well, all things considered, I'm pretty sick of
keeping myself on a leash."

He cupped her face, and in the dim light he could see that she
was staring up at him, her eyes wide. And then, without letting
another breath go by, he dipped his head and his lips crushed up
against Jamie Dodge's.

They were soft.

Good God, she was soft.

He didn't know what he had expected.

Prickles, maybe.

But no, her lips were the softest, sweetest thing he'd felt in
a long time. It was like a flash of light had gone off and erased
everything in his brain, like all his thoughts had been printed on
an old-school film roll.

There was nothing.

Nothing beyond the sensation of her skin beneath his
fingertips, the feel of her mouth under his. She was frozen
beneath his touch, and he shifted, tilting his head to the side and
darting his tongue out, flicking it against the seam of her lips.

She gasped, and he took advantage of that, getting entry into that pretty mouth so he could taste her, deep and long, and exactly how he'd been fantasizing about.

Oh, those fantasies hadn't been a fully realized scroll of images. No. It had been a feeling.

An invisible band of tension that had stretched between them in small spaces of time. In the leap of panic in his heart when he'd seen her fall from the horse earlier today.

It had been embedded in all of those things and he hadn't realized exactly what it meant he wanted until the right moment. And then suddenly it was like her shock transformed into something else entirely.

She arched toward him, her breasts pressing against his chest, her hands coming up to his face. She thrust her chin upward, making the kiss harder, deeper. He drove his tongue deep, sliding it against hers, and she made a small sound like a whimpering kitten. The smallest sound he'd ever heard Jamie Dodge make.

He pulled away from her, nipped her lower lip and then pressed his mouth to hers one more time before releasing his hold.

She looked dazed. He felt about how she looked.

"I thought about it," he said. "And I realized I couldn't let this one go. I let you criticize my riding, question my authority, but I wasn't about to let you get away with cock-blocking me, telling me you're jealous and then telling me you don't know if you want me. So I figured maybe I'd give you something to think about."

Don't miss
Cowboy to the Core *by Maisey Yates,*
available July 2019 wherever
Harlequin® books and ebooks are sold.

www.Harlequin.com

*Dealing with her insufferable hotshot boss has
India Crowley at the breaking point. But when he faces
a stand-in daddy dilemma, India can't deny him a
helping hand. Sharing close quarters, though,
may mean facing her true feelings about the man...*

Read on for a sneak peek at
BIG SHOT
by New York Times *bestselling author Katy Evans!*

hate my boss

My demanding, stone-hearted, arrogant bastard boss.

You know those people in an elevator who click the close
button repeatedly when they see someone coming just to
avoid human contact? You know what?

That's my boss. But worse.

As I settle in, I notice that my boss, William, isn't around.

He's the kind of person who turns up early to work for
no good reason. It's probably because he has no social life—
he's a lone wolf, according to my mother, but to me, that
translates as he's a jerk with no friends. Despite the lackeys
who follow him around everywhere, I know he doesn't have
any real friends. After all, I control his calendar for personal
appointments, and in truth, there aren't many.

But where is he today? Not being early is like being late
for him. Until he arrives, there's little I can do, so I meander
to the coffee machine and make a cup for myself. As the

machine is churning up coffee beans, the elevator dings and William appears.

I'll admit, something about his presence always knock the breath from me. He stalks forward, with three peopl following in his wake. His hair is perfectly slicked, his stubbl trimmed close to his sharp jaw. His eyes are a shocking blue I can picture him now on the front cover of *Business Insider* his piercing eyes radiating confidence from the page. Bu today his eyes are clouded by anger.

He spots me waiting. The whole office is watching as h stalks toward me with a bunch of papers in his arms. Hi colleagues struggle to keep up, and I discard my coffee suddenly fearful of his glare. Did I do something wrong?

"Good morning, Mr. Walker—"

"Good morning, India," he growls.

He shoves the papers into my arms and I almost toppl over in surprise. "I need you to sort out this paperwork mes and I don't want to hear another word from you until it' done." When he stalks away without so much as a smile, notice I've been holding my breath.

And this is why, despite his beauty, despite his money despite his drive, I can't stand the man.

Will she feel the same way when
they're in close quarters? Find out in
BIG SHOT
by New York Times *bestselling author Katy Evans.*

Available August 2019 wherever
Harlequin® Desire books and ebooks are sold.

www.Harlequin.com